THE SPY WITH HIS HEAD
IN THE CLOUDS

By Marc Lovell

THE SPY WITH HIS HEAD IN THE CLOUDS
THE SPY GAME
HAND OVER MIND
A VOICE FROM THE LIVING
THE SECOND VANETTI AFFAIR
THE BLIND HYPNOTIST
DREAMERS IN A HAUNTED HOUSE
AN ENQUIRY INTO THE EXISTENCE OF VAMPIRES
A PRESENCE IN THE HOUSE
THE IMITATION THIEVES
THE GHOST OF MEGAN

THE SPY
WITH HIS HEAD
IN THE CLOUDS

MARC LOVELL

PUBLISHED FOR THE CRIME CLUB BY
DOUBLEDAY & COMPANY, INC.
GARDEN CITY, NEW YORK
1982

All of the characters in this book
are fictitious, and any resemblance
to actual persons, living or dead,
is purely coincidental.

First Edition

Library of Congress Catalog Card Number 81-43281
Copyright © 1982 by Doubleday & Company, Inc.
All Rights Reserved
Printed in the United States of America

THE SPY WITH HIS HEAD IN THE CLOUDS

CHAPTER 1

When Apple got the sensation that he was being followed, he began to slow. Next, he came to a stop by a store window, into which he looked. His hands he clasped behind him as an aid in creating a picture of the absorbed browser.

So intent was Apple on trying to gauge the strength of his sensation of being tailed that several seconds passed before he realized the window's emptiness in respect of goods. It held only a single, naked mannikin.

Great start, Apple thought. You're doing fine. A real pro.

After straightening his tie and smoothing a lapel, as if he had been using the window as a mirror, Apple turned away and moved on. His dark suit was immaculate. Nothing about him needed putting to rights. But he didn't think about it, for he would only get depressed.

Apple often wished he had the nerve to buy wild clothes, or a trench coat, or a suit that was less respectable. Even a slouch hat would have been something, but that would have added to his height.

Appleton Porter was six feet seven inches tall—barefooted. Now there was another half inch on top of that, his shoes having the minimum of heel. His sandy hair, neatly cut, was kept flat on top with oil. Every trick in the reduction of height was known to him and used.

It wasn't only Apple's thin tallness that depressed him. He

looked, he knew, altogether mundane and reliable, with his paleness, passable good-looks, and freckles. What he wanted to look was dangerous, perhaps cruel, a bastard to women and a two-fisted drinker. It would have made him happy to be treated by people with caution, or even outright distrust. Instead, children asked him the time, pretty girls stood near him in railway stations, and policemen glanced at him with approval.

Apple strolled on along Oxford Street, heading east. Defensively he told himself that looking at naked female dummies in shop windows was the most natural thing in the world for a man to do. All men did, in fact, do it, though usually from the corners of their eyes. So, hadn't he been demonstrating what an open, unsly, straightforward sort of person he was?

This, Apple decided, was true, which meant that looking in the window had been an extremely shrewd bit of business. If, that is, there was anyone behind for the bit to impress.

He still had the sensation. It was a faint prickling at the base of his spine, across the shoulders, behind the ears. It could have been due to the chill breeze that was cooling this morning in early June, but Apple refused to accept that. He did know, as he had learned in Training Four, that he should never presume. Meaning: Yes, someone could be watching him and moving in the same direction. The interest, however, could be innocent—ranging from the follower mistaking him for somebody else, to . . .

Apple couldn't remember the others. His memory, except for the visual, was less than average for an operative, though by cribbing and faking during tests he had managed to score eight out of ten. Apple knew all his scores by heart. He had bribed a secretary with gin and flattery to get them for him from Upstairs.

10	Languages
10	Security clearance

6	Unarmed combat
6	Acting ability
6	Inventiveness in lying
5	Resistance to physical pain
9	Resistance to mental stress
9	General knowledge
7	Marksmanship
5	Tolerance for alcohol

A pub, Apple mused. Maybe he should go in a bar and see if anyone followed him in. A glance at his watch told him it was only a quarter to eleven: Licenced premises weren't open yet.

Unavoidingly, annoyingly, his mind went back to that list. In itself, it had satisfied him. What had sent his spirits sinking had been the words beneath, under the heading REMARKS. In red ink, REMARKS damned him with *Has a sympathetic nature and is inclined to blush.*

To stop himself from blushing now, in recollection of that libel—true, alas—Apple quickly pictured himself sitting in a sauna, wearing a fur coat. Due to the theory of competition in heat, it worked, just as the advertiser had claimed it would, or money would be refunded within seven days. Apple bought through magazine ads all his cures for blushing, none of which were good for more than a month or two, familiarity weakening effect.

Apple moved to the curb. He liked the uncertainty about whether or not he had a tail, but thought he ought to be reacting more forcefully. That might be the reason he was taking this apparently pointless stroll along Oxford Street.

He stopped and looked back. At once, among the moving mass of shoppers on this side, he picked out a possible. The man, in a grey suit and a chauffeur's cap, had come to a halt while Apple was turning. Now he drew a newspaper from his pocket, looked at it with his head lowered, moved slowly out of sight among the crowd.

Bloody amateur, Apple thought. Feeling clever, he got out his cigarettes and lit up with a flourish. He refused to believe that the man could be genuine. He was determined to get the most out of this outing, whatever it might be.

All Apple knew was from a short telephone call. It had come this morning while he was breakfasting in the screaming tartan robe that he enjoyed wearing in private. The caller had been his Control, Angus Watkin, though he used a number instead of a name. He had said in his dull brown voice:

"I don't intend to repeat myself, Porter. Listen and note. I want you, at ten-thirty, to go for a walk along Oxford Street, in any direction you wish. The give-word is Hamnett, the response is Sickert. They were actors, I believe, in case you should waste time on puzzling about that."

Apple knew they were artists but had said, "I see, sir." It was best not to contradict Angus Watkin. "What do I do next, please?"

"Good-bye, Porter."

There was no sign of the man in the chauffeur's cap. Apple dropped his cigarette in the gutter and walked on.

He was intrigued by the choice of code-words. While he himself liked the Service slang, and all of its romantic trimmings, Angus Watkin was primly opposed to the use of any kind of cant. But Hamnett and Sickert were curiously close to the slang terms for male and female KGB agents—Hammer and Sickle.

Most intriguing, Apple thought. He turned into a side street and began to stride swiftly.

There were few people about. Apple was able to move without hindrance. At the next corner he made another left, then started running. With his long legs, he was a good runner. He couldn't help smiling. He felt free and vital and happy.

Swinging left again at the next corner, he went on until he was back on Oxford Street, where he slowed to a normal walking pace. Being tall, he was able to see well ahead in the crowd. He looked for a cap among the bobbing heads. He could see none.

Apple passed the side street, kept on. Neither in doorways nor elsewhere was there any sign of the man. As Apple turned to look behind, he recalled the trick of first establishing an image with a particularly noticeable piece of clothing or carried object, and then getting rid of it.

But it was too late. When Apple turned back again, having seen nothing, he found the man. He was walking quietly at his side. The chauffeur's cap had gone.

Apple said nothing. He felt stupid, felt the amateur he really was. After a moment he slowed to an amble. With him slowed the man, who was so average looking and ordinary, except for a mild scar on one cheek, that Apple got a pang of envy.

"Excuse me," he said, voice cool.

The man looked up at him as if he were a signpost warning of a dead-end. "Yes?"

"There's a Nina Hamnett retrospective showing somewhere around here. Perhaps you could tell me where it is."

"Sorry. It's the Walter Sickert show I'm looking for."

They both came to a halt. Apple asked, "What now?"

"A drink," the agent said. "Follow me."

Apple did, meekly. He was low and worried. If this was a test, he thought, one which might have put him into active service, surely he must have failed.

Only once in his employment by British Intelligence had Apple been out in the espionage field. REMARKS was against

5

him, as well as a height that made him stand out anywhere. His work had been restricted to his gift for languages. He spoke six fluently, five with competence but an accent, and had a sound knowledge of seven more. He was a senior official at the United Kingdom Philological Institute. No one there, at that Kensington mansion, knew about his other work.

It was, in any case, an occasional thing, one that took up little of his time. He went over decoded transcriptions, looking for nuance and word-play. As a simultaneous translator he sat in on high-shelf military conferences. He wrote letters, playing anything from a businessman to a heart-scarred lover. He gave his opinion on if a suspect's language was original with him or acquired.

Apple knew that there were many like himself attached to the secret services. These faceless ones each had a speciality that might be needed no more than once a year, or once in a career-life: coin-faker, pickpocket, sniper, cat-burglar. They were invaluable—but rarely. They were not so much cloak and dagger, Apple often thought glumly, as cape and penknife.

He followed the agent in grey down an alley and into a pub. It had just opened. There were no other customers. The room was drab, with cracked linoleum and a smoke-yellowed ceiling. The dart-board looked to have taken a shotgun blast. There were four separate signs saying that credit wasn't given. The place smelled of drains.

An overpainted barmaid appeared, her head cocked in query. The man said, "A pint of bitter for me, please, and a sherry on the rocks for my friend."

That his favourite drink was known to the agent made Apple sigh. Though only his own age, near thirty, the man was obviously well up the ladder. He would not, otherwise, have had access to such dossier details.

In a try at asserting himself, Apple said, "There's a theory, by the way, that Sickert knew the identity of Jack the Ripper. He's supposed to have put clues in many of his later paintings."

The agent turned to him slowly. "Oh?" he said. He looked away again.

Apple told himself that, while the habit of collecting trivia was harmless in itself, he should make an effort to refrain from passing it on. He said, "So I've heard."

The agent was busy counting out coins. The barmaid took them and rang the till. She left.

Apple said dismally, "Cheers."

The man looked up at him. "You don't know what this is all about, do you?"

"No, I don't."

"Well, to begin with, I'm going to give you three telephone numbers. You have to commit them to memory. Ready?"

Nodding, Apple closed his eyes. He repeated each number aloud and then visualised it as a collection of digits. He hoped the images would remain. Opening his eyes he lied, "That was easy enough."

"Good. Now look at that top line of bottles. See if you can fix the sequence of labels."

Apple stared across the bar. There were ten bottles and he knew that he would remember the sequence later, and for long afterwards.

"Your health," the agent said. He lifted his pint and drained off a third. With his wrinkled shirt, plain tie and ready-made suit, he could have passed for a clerk sneaking out for a mid-morning beer.

Apple sipped his drink. "What else?"

"No hurry. I'll tell you in a minute. Let's knock these back

7

and get 'em in again. It's on my expense account. You can have a Scotch, if you like."

"This is fine."

Smilingly, the agent mused aloud, "I wonder what they'd say if I bought a bottle of champers."

"You might get fired."

"Old Angus wouldn't do that. Not unless his ulcer was acting up. How did he look when you saw him this morning?"

Apple drained his glass. "Didn't. He called me."

"Who called you?"

Apple paused. He said to the agent, who was looking at him with a face void of expression, "Why, Angus, of course."

"Angus who?"

Apple let his second pause grow long. Carefully he said, "The same Angus you just mentioned." This, he thought, is odd. Is the man drunk? Is he trying to trap me, or have I already been trapped?

"I didn't use any names."

"All right, you didn't. Forget it."

"How about another drink?" the agent asked. His forehead began to swell. It came out to the size of a football. After holding there briefly, it shrank again, and went on shrinking. He was left with a flatness that began level with his eyebrows.

"I'm dreaming," Apple said, relieved but at the same time disappointed. "I knew it was too good to be true."

The man's head had gone. His voice, coming out of the empty shirt collar, said, "I think you'd better sit down."

The chair was comfortable. He felt nice and relaxed. He was in the focus of an array of lights, which were brilliantly bright. Behind them, vaguely, he could see the upper silhouettes of men, five or six. They were friendly, he knew that beyond any doubt. They had made him at home and were letting him have all this marvellous lighting.

A voice spoke. It had an attractive harsh quality. It asked, "How long have you worked for British Intelligence?"

"Eight or nine years," Apple said. "Since coming down from university." It made him happy to be able to help these people, his friends, to show how much he appreciated their interest in him.

"You were recruited there?"

"Yes, by my don. Another professor, Atwater, was recruiting for the Communists. He still is. And so is my old don—recruiting for us, I mean."

"Just answer the questions."

"Of course. I'm terribly sorry. Do tell me if I'm boring you."

The harsh voice asked, "Your cover is the UK Philological Institute?"

"Well, yes, but it's also a real job."

"Your superior's name?"

"Warden. A marvellous old chap. He speaks fourteen languages fluently but can never think of the word he wants in English."

"Which of the secret services are you attached to?"

"Not any particular one," Apple said. "And I've never been Upstairs. I don't even know where the building is. I suppose you could say I'm freelance, except my lance is so free it's hardly ever used."

"This is no occasion for levity."

Apple shuffled himself. He swallowed. He hoped he hadn't offended anyone. That would be unforgivable. What a way to return hospitality. "I'm sorry," he said.

"There is a building you do know of. In the country. What is it called?"

"Damian House. Its cover is that it's a holiday home for armed services personnel and their families, but actually it's used as a rest home and training centre for operatives. I've been there several times."

"Then you may give us details."

Apple did. He gave all he knew—staff, security, exact location, heads of departments. He felt more wonderful by the minute, not only because of being able to help, but from feeling so physically fine. It was as if his head were in the clouds, even though he knew he was firmly in a chair and in a large room with a beamed ceiling.

When Apple had exhausted the subject of Damian House, the nicely harsh voice spoke again. It came from the head-and-shoulders shape that was nearer than the others. It asked:

"If you don't know where Upstairs is, how do you go about making contact, when that's necessary?"

"I have a telephone number," Apple said. He gave it. "The man who answers says I must have misdialled, and what number was I trying to get. I tell him one. The first three digits identify me, the rest identify the person to whom I wish to speak." He gave the digits. "If he's not there, the telephonist says yes, I misdialled."

"Who is that second person? Your Control?"

"Yes. Angus Watkin."

"Describe him."

Apple obliged. The voice asked, "Do you like him?"

"Not particularly. He's prim and fussy, is old Angus. No sense of humour whatever. A bit of a cold fish. He enjoys being mysterious when he could just as easily tell his underlings what's going on. I don't know if anyone likes him, and I'm not saying that because he hardly ever sends me out in the field. It's true."

"Why doesn't he use you more often, do you think?"

Earnestly, Apple explained about his height. "In addition to that, there's my soft-hearted ways, as some see it, and this thing I have of blushing."

"You could have tried faking in the tests."

"I did on the memory course, but the others were found out about during what's called Social Activities. I'm not supposed to know of it, but I do."

"How did you find out?"

"Very easily, as a matter of fact. There was this secretary from Upstairs. I took her out for a drink. I'd met her when I was on a courier mission—it lasted all of thirty minutes. Anyway, I got this girl, her name's Jenny North, to copy my report and show it to me."

The voice asked, "What would happen to her if anyone found out what she had done?"

"I wouldn't like to guess, poor girl," Apple said. "She lives with an aunt and has thick ankles. She's plain. I lied to her. I told her she was beautiful." He felt a lump growing in his throat at the thought of having lied to someone.

The voice said, "You were one of the translators last month on a conference between French and British naval people. Is that not so?"

Apple nodded until he got his emotions under control. "Yes. It was at Portsmouth. The discussion was about a submarine. It was Top, Very, and Most Secret." He smiled proudly. "My security clearance is ten out of ten."

"You are to be congratulated."

"Thank you."

"Your superiors, therefore, know that you would never breathe a word of what you heard, and translated, at that conference."

"They do indeed."

"Excellent," the charmingly harsh voice said. "So go ahead and tell us exactly what was said at the conference table."

"Gladly. With the greatest of pleasure. There's rather a lot of it, so it might be better if you took notes. I'll go slowly. Also there were plans. I'll try to draw them for you afterwards, but I can't be sure how close I'll get to the originals. But I'll do my very best, be assured of that. My very, very best."

Apple came awake slowly. He slipped comfortably in and out of stretches of dozing. Between, he noted mistily that above him was a caged light bulb. It glared starkly. What, he began to question, was that doing on the ceiling of a pub?

Apple left his last doze behind. Breathing deeply for the oxygen, he lay still, on his back, and looked carefully all around. He soon saw that not only was this not the bar in which he had felt faint, but nor could it be another room somewhere in that same pub. Not, that is, unless the pub had a peculiar business of some kind on the side.

Ceiling and walls were concrete. The door was solid wood and had a Judas-hole. There was no window. By the prickly feel of it, what he lay on was a thin, straw-filled mattress, it was placed directly on the floor, also of concrete. He was in a cell.

Stunned, Apple got to his feet. He looked down at himself, felt his hair and tie and pockets. He was as neat as usual and nothing had been taken from him. So he hadn't been rolled. Neither was he in pain. Neither did he feel sick.

Cautiously Apple moved to the door. There was nothing to be heard from the other side. There was no handle he could try. About to knock, he decided it would be best first to weigh form. He got out his cigarettes, lit up, and drew hungrily at the smoke.

Feeling brighter, even amused by the strange circumstances, Apple thought back. He remembered the pub, the agent, the drink, the talk that seemed to get a little odd, and then— nothing.

Could it be, he mused, that the sherry had gone straight to his head? That he had drunk others and staggered out, been picked up by the police, and brought here to a common cell? No, because in that case he would be feeling rotten. He felt fine.

Could the sherry have been drugged? No, too dramatic, at least when considered in connexion with an operative of his own low standing. Also, there would be an after-effect.

Apple frowned and clopped his tongue against the roof of his mouth. He tasted, faintly, a strawberry flavour. It became stronger when he sucked on his teeth.

So maybe a drug couldn't be ruled out, he thought. Not that he knew of any that left behind an essence of strawberries, and he'd had a thorough grounding in narcotics during Training Seven. But that was years ago, and new drugs were coming out all the time. It could be.

The agent in the grey suit? He couldn't be on the other side because he had owned the code-word. On the other hand, he had started to talk oddly.

Apple dropped his cigarette and ground it out underfoot. He put his fingertips to his temples and worked at remembering what had been said. It was, he felt, something about a name.

He gave up. One thing he did know for sure, he thought, looking around: This was no holiday camp. He hadn't been brought here to improve his health or spirits. He was somebody's prisoner.

Apple stepped back to the door. He rapped. The wood was so thick and hard that there was almost no sound—and his knuckles hurt. He thumped with the side of his fist. That wasn't much better as a noise-maker.

Standing back, Apple raised his right leg and sent out a hard kick, making his shoe land flat. The result was a satisfying boom, plus a shuddering of the door. He kicked again.

Every few seconds, over a period of two minutes, Apple crashed the flat of his shoe against the door. He stopped because he became out of breath, which he knew meant he had been smoking too much today. He sat on the mattress to rest, shot up again at once on hearing the distant tap of footsteps.

Listening acutely, he heard the taps come closer, then stop at the door. There was the sound of a bolt being drawn. Giving a squeal from a Dracula movie, the door began to open, coming inward. With it came a man.

He was short and of early middle age, hair fluffy with sparcity. His eyes were tired, his face sunken. He wore a blue coverall and white running shoes.

"Well," he began and got no further, for Apple flung himself forward. He grappled and pushed.

They stumbled out into a dim hallway. Moving himself clear, Apple brought down a whistling karate chop. It went through air and he hit himself on the thigh.

Next, he was lying on his back.

Angry, he leapt up. He sent out a parrying left. The man, standing calmly, grabbed the hand as if snatching at a fly. He held on and put his other hand on Apple's wrist.

"Now now," he said, his tone gentle.

Apple found himself unable to move. He was stooping from the waist. In the man's two-handed hold, which didn't hurt, his arm seemed to be void of feeling, as though it were asleep and would start tingling any second now. His head was almost resting on the man's shoulder.

Apple gasped, "Where did you learn that?"

"Kindergarten," the man said. His accent was Cockney. "They

14

didn't take you quite that far at Damian House, did they?"

"Eh?"

"Now come along quietly, as the coppers say." Without loosing his hold, he turned so that he was beside Apple, who stayed in his stoop as they went along the passage and up a flight of steps. They came into a hallway, typical of a London townhouse. The man took Apple along to a door, releasing him there with:

"Now behave. You're all right."

He knocked. From inside, a voice mumbled. The man jerked his head. Apple, still in the act of straightening up, opened the door and went through.

It was a pleasant room, the window looking out onto a walled garden. Chintz-covered couch and easy chairs were arranged around a coffee table. Books lined the walls. The man who was standing, back turned, at the tea trolley, was carefully pouring tea.

Tiredly, Apple said, "Good morning, sir."

Angus Watkin turned. "It's two sugars, isn't it, Porter?"

Birds squabbled in the garden, sunlight slanted down prettily through the window, there was a hum of distant traffic. It was all reassuring to Apple, who sat at his ease on the couch, sipping tea. The sole reminders of his recent experience were restricted to his encounter with the coveralled man: a pain in his thigh from his own karate chop, an ache in the small of his back from the enforced stooping.

Apple stopped gazing around the room when Watkin said, "No, Porter. This is not what some of you people so quaintly call Upstairs. It's a house in Notting Hill, which we use for certain activities."

Angus Watkin sat in an armchair, the cup and saucer held

close to his chest. He was average height, slightly plump, aged between fifty and sixty. His face was unremarkable. It was smooth except for a ridge across his top lip that showed he had worn a moustache for many years. He had neat brown hair. His eyes were sleepy, showing neither intelligence nor alertness. Altogether, he looked like someone who would be boring if given any encouragement.

For the second time Watkin asked, "Albert didn't hurt you?"

"No, sir. He's too skilled for that, obviously."

"But you tried your best, I hope."

"Oh yes," Apple said. "I thought he was an enemy and I intended to put him out of action."

"So it was his skill that won the day, not the fact that you weren't feeling at your best."

"Exactly, sir. I felt fine. I still do."

"I'm delighted to hear it," Angus Watkin said. He finished his tea, set cup and saucer tidily on the table. "You have no headache, no nausea, no dizziness? Good. When you awoke, there was no trauma at finding yourself in a strange place?"

Apple said, "Trauma, no. A bit of worry, yes. But that was only natural. After all, I couldn't figure out the score."

"Precisely," Watkin said. "And how about when you were kicking the door—did that jolt you physically any more than it would have done normally?"

"I don't think so, sir."

The host waved a hand, as if scattering alms to the wretched. "You may smoke, if you wish."

Apple put down his cup and got out cigarettes. He knew better than to offer one to his superior. After lighting up he said, "I was either drugged or hypnotised."

"A drug," Watkin said. "And you're quite sure there are no after-effects? No sluggishness? No dryness in the mouth?"

"Well, sir, there was a slight taste. It's gone now. It had a strawberry flavour."

Watkin looked pleased, like a housewife who finds dust when the maid's left. "That's interesting. But had you awoken under different circumstances, your own bed for instance, do you think you would have noticed the taste?"

"I'm sure I shouldn't. It was too faint."

"Splendid," Angus Watkin said. He got up, collected the crockery, and put it on the tea trolley. Apple could have done with a second cup, but didn't dare suggest it. Back in his chair Watkin said:

"Having dispensed with aftermath, we now come to overture. Tell me about your morning, please."

Apple began with the telephone call, ended with being in the pub with the agent. Between, he embroidered on the truth with, "I circled, came up behind him and fell into step at his side." Every bit helped.

Angus Watkin seemed uninterested. He asked, "You and he exchanged the correct code-words—Hammer and Sickle?"

"No, sir. The words you gave me on the telephone were Hamnett and Sickert. We exchanged those."

Unperturbed: "In the pub he gave you three six-digit numbers. What were they, please?"

Apple was prepared. While drinking his tea, closing his eyes as if against the steam, he had brought back the image of the numbers, which he now recited. He had begun to see what the outing was about.

Angus Watkin checked a slip of paper. "Correct. Now the sequence of bottle labels, please."

Apple rattled off what had been easy because it was visual. His confidence became stronger. He was sure now that this had been a test, and that he had passed it with colours that, if not exactly flying, weren't sagging on the staff.

"Good," Watkin said. After putting the slip of paper away—Apple could imagine him destroying it methodically later—he clasped his hands and leaned forward slightly.

"The drug was, of course, administered by the operative. He's an expert at sleight-of-hand."

And brought into service once a year? Apple wondered. He said, "He was very smooth."

"So I understand."

"And, by the way, he was just as smooth at tailing. He knew what I was up to." He felt better for saying that.

Covering a twitch of impatience, Watkin said, "Yes, I'm sure. But the drug. Did you suspect what had happened when you felt faint?"

"No, and that was only for a second or two. My last memory is of a misunderstanding over names."

Almost smiling faintly, Angus Watkin settled back in the chair. He nodded. "Well, Porter," he said, "I do apologise for the rigmarole, but you'll understand soon that it was necessary. It wasn't done for fun and frolic. A lot of work went into setting this up."

"I think I do understand, sir," Apple said—and realized he had made a mistake. His superior enjoyed being able to enlighten. He went on, "But it's only a suspicion, and what I can't figure out is how you got me here from the pub. That must have been tricky."

"Actually, quite simple. After a minute of grogginess you were able to walk, guided. You were helped into a car and brought here."

"Then put into a strange place to sleep it off," Apple said, "so that my recovery could be gauged accurately."

"That came later," Watkin said, and Apple could tell by an eyelid flicker that his superior had not only recuperated from having to admit lack of cleverness in the exit from the pub but had climbed the other way.

Apple helped with, "Later, sir?"

Angus Watkin put his hands on his knees and levered himself up with a murmur of effort. He said, "Let's have a stroll downstairs, shall we, Porter?"

The whitewashed room was bare except for the bank of electronic equipment that covered one wall. As in the cell, which lay farther along the same corridor, the lighting was stark.

Apple stood by the bank, beside Watkin, who now asked an ominously careless, "Ready?"

"Yes, sir."

"The first voice you hear, and will hear throughout, you will not know. It was agreed that you might recognise mine, if I tried to disguise it, and be influenced accordingly. The second voice will be more than familiar to you."

Although Apple had no liking for any of this, he acted an alert, "I see, sir."

Watkin reached out and pressed down a switch. From the speakers came a harsh, unpleasant voice. It ordered, "Tell us your name."

Apple would not have recognised himself as the responder, not at once, had it not been for the matter. His tone was like that of someone talking in his sleep, pale and distant:

"Appleton Porter. My friends call me Apple. There are others who call me Russet, which I don't care for. They use it because—"

"Just answer the questions."

"Of course. Please excuse me."

The harsh voice asked, "How long have you worked for British Intelligence?"

Apple, with growing horror, listened to himself answer correctly. He recovered partway on remembering who the questioners were, and that he had been drugged. But he was still unhappy.

Next, he heard himself tell about Professor Warden, give away all the secrets of Damian House, and explain how he made contact with Upstairs. He stood in a miserable crouch, head down, hands tightly clasped, while Angus Watkin teetered amiably on his toes, hands behind, his gaze airily on the wall. He might have been listening to a string quartet.

"Not particularly. He's prim and fussy, is old Angus. No sense of humour whatever. A bit of a cold fish. He enjoys . . ."

The horror came back. And Apple began to blush. The heat zoomed up him from his groin, burning its way like flames. It was one of the worst attacks he had ever known. His face scorched and tingled, his ears throbbed, his neck turned wet.

I am in a sauna, he thought desperately, trying with the thought to keep out his taped voice, which was going on cheerfully maligning his superior. I am in a steaming sauna and I am wearing a fur coat.

It didn't work. The blush flared on, proudly, like a beacon for the brave. Apple suffered. He cringed and swayed and let one clasped hand fight the other. Sweat ran down from his neck.

Angus Watkin was still appreciating the string quartet, still teetering on his toes. Now he began to hum—lightly. His face showed nothing.

You bastard, Apple thought from inside his blush. You rotten, cruel bastard.

On the tape, the subject of Angus Watkin finished. Apple was beginning to win over his red attack, until he heard his recorded self start telling how he had faked the memory course.

I am in a sauna, Apple fumed. As well as wearing a fur coat I have a woollen hat, thick gloves, and a scarf.

Apple kept this up over the next few minutes, over his explaining how he got his file with the help of Jenny North, over his recounting of what had been said at the naval conference. He added fur boots, an electric blanket, and two hot-water bottles. Somehow, he survived.

There seemed to be more to come, but Watkin switched off. Next he pressed another switch and the speakers gave a high-pitched squiggling like a whistling competition in the distance. Ending that, he said:

"The tape is now erased. We have to do this because the information you gave was one hundred per cent accurate. Which means that the drug is one hundred per cent efficacious."

Apple worked at recovery. His blush had completely gone. He felt as white as he supposed he looked. He was cool from his sodden shirt.

"Obviously," Watkin went on, "the evil-sounding voice, the uncomfortable chair and those painfully strong lights made no difference. You accepted it all, and gladly."

Apple nodded. He felt unable to speak.

"You proved to my complete satisfaction, Porter, that we can make marvellous use of this drug, because of its almost nonexistent warning qualities and after-effects, plus, most important of all, its ability to blot out any recollection of what went on during the drug-state. You see the possibilities?"

Apple managed a "Yes, sir."

As if he hadn't heard, still gazing at the wall—for which Apple was thankful—Watkin said, "The number-one possibility is that we can pick up a Communist agent, get the marrow truth from him, put him back in favourable circumstances, and he'll never know a thing about it."

"Quite, sir. I get your point now." He was pleased with himself at having the sense to play the toady. "I didn't quite see it before."

"You also see, I hope, why we had to go through all that rigmarole earlier today—Oxford Street and so forth. The drug had to have a thorough test. If we had used an operative who was widely experienced in the field, who had the slightest suspicion —and operatives are, by trade, suspicious—we couldn't have been sure of the results. We are now. At the moment, anyway, if not next week."

"Sir?"

"I mean to say, for all we know you could drop dead in a few days. There might be a long-term effect."

"Oh."

Angus Watkin said, "The reason we chose you, Porter, is because you have the highest security rating possible, as well as a very high score in resistance to psychological persuasion. In addition to the fact, of course, that you speak Hungarian."

He brought his gaze around, which was the only sign that he had made himself happy by being surprising.

Apple said, "I speak it with an accent, sir."

Again as if he hadn't heard, Watkin said, looking at Apple's shoulder, "I think I ought to mention, in passing, that Jenny North is no longer in the Service. We can't rap her knuckles."

That, at least, was something, Apple thought. He straightened with relief. "I—er—don't know what to say about that, sir."

"Furthermore, Jenny is married. To a chum of mine, actually. He doesn't think she's plain, nor have I ever heard him complain about her ankles."

Apple whispered, "No, sir."

Watkin said, "And, Porter, as to your remarks about myself. I have been slandered by international experts in venom. Your assault was rather feeble."

Another whisper: "Yes, sir. I hope so, sir."

His superior turned toward the door. "Come along. We're going for a drive."

The car, plain black, was as anonymous as the street it stood in, although the parking metre, Apple noted, was fully paid up for the next two hours. He wondered if it ever showed empty.

Angus Watkin followed him inside, onto the back seat. He slammed the door and said, "Off we go, Albert."

The man in the coverall, after saluting with a raised finger, set the car in motion. He touched a knob on the dashboard, saying, "There you are, sir."

Apple saw tiny lights come to life, on a rod running across the top of the front seat. They were green, spaced an inch apart, and gave off no more glow than the bulbs on a Christmas tree.

"New gadget," Angus Watkin said. "Don't ask me how, but they kill every word we say. Even Albert can't hear."

Apple nodded with unfeigned interest. He loved gadgetry. However, he had always suspected that it didn't really exist to an extensive degree in the secret services. "Marvellous."

"But the trouble is, the damn thing keeps breaking down, and usually when I want to show it off to someone."

Apple wondered, as he sometimes had before, if after all there could be a trace of humanity somewhere in his superior. He took that back when the other man added:

"Fortunately, it's seldom I have anyone of consequence riding in this car."

Albert smoothly swung them into the traffic on a main road. Apple guessed that the driver was one of those people who had so many valuable skills that they worked on a permanent basis. Which made him think about his own mission today. He looked sharply at his superior.

Watkin caught the glance. "Yes," he said. "Quite right. Time I got on with it. And I'll begin, I believe, by telling you about a party. It took place some days ago. Where, that doesn't matter for the moment. It was a party for about a hundred people and everybody had a scintillating time. Established?"

"Yes, sir," Apple said. He was hoping hard.

"It wasn't much of a drinking type of thing, more a feast, with silly hats and streamers and false noses. The celebrants ate a lot and played games. They also did their party-pieces: a song, a tune on an instrument, and so forth. It was the kind of occasion, in fact, that would probably make me feel ill.

"The hit of the evening was performed by a man whom we shall call Tom. He gave a girl something to drink, told her it was a powerful drug that would make her tell the truth, and then proceeded to ask her a great many questions. The girl did tell the truth, apparently, with hilarious results. She was talking about the people present, many of whom didn't like these truths, particularly the host, who was the one our Tom harped on most. But all in all, it was funny and popular, and no one thought much about it afterwards."

"They took it," Apple said, "that the girl had been hypnotised."

Watkin nodded. "Exactly. But a certain person there, he quietly, at party time, lifted the pop bottle the drink had been in, and which still filled it to the two-thirds mark. That bottle landed on my desk."

Apple said, "If it had been full to begin with, the dose would seem to be a third."

"That, yes, was our assumption. Therefore we gave half the

remains to a volunteer. The results were excellent but not without doubts. That's where you came into the picture. You, Porter, were given the final dose."

Emphasising the plural pronoun, Apple asked, "We haven't got any more?"

Angus Watkin slowly shook his head. "Not a drop."

The car turned onto Edgware Road. Apple wondered dismally if he were being driven home. He said with force, "But we know the man who gave it to the girl."

"We think we do. Someone might have given it to *him*. But yes, that's an easy one. Tom is probably our man. The stumbling block is, however, he might deny having anything to do with the drug. You see, it's possible that he uses it, illegally, in his profession. "

"So he has to be handled with kid gloves."

Watkin was silent for a moment, looking out of the window. Turning to Apple, who had noticed happily through the same window that they had passed his turn-off, he said in a solemn voice:

"We of the Service have an unwritten law. It states that anyone who has suffered during a mission must be in at the climax. Equally, anyone who has suffered in a mission's early stages must have the opportunity of working further on it. Therefore, Porter, I am bound by honour to offer you this piece of fieldwork."

Or, Apple thought to control his excitement, it's a gift because I might drop dead next week. Or because this is a risky one and Appleton Porter is expendable.

He said coolly, "I see, sir. But . . ."

"The other agent? The volunteer drug-taker? Yes, he should have been asked as well. However, he's a bit under the weather. Some kind of bug that's going around."

There was another silence. Apple told himself it didn't matter, for there was no way he could untake the drug. He would, at least, be working at the end. He said, so as not to appear overeager:

"I'd have to fix it at the Institute."

"That's already been taken care of," Watkin said, "to save time, on the chance that you might accept the mission. If you don't, you can easily take back the story, which is that you've gone to the funeral of a relative up North."

"I'm from the West."

"But it's not you that's dead, Porter."

"Quite, sir," Apple said, quickly because of the hint of testiness in the other man's tone. "And I accept the job."

Watkin drawled a hand movement. "You may smoke." He waited until Apple had a cigarette going before saying briskly, "In a few minutes we will arrive at a garage. It's safe. I shall give you the rest of the story, along with a cup of tea. Into an envelope you will place all identification. Labels in clothes don't matter—you will be using your own name. You will be given new papers, which will show that you're a market gardener from Kent. That end is tight, should there be a check. I'm not going too fast for you, am I, Porter?"

Despite a shade of dryness in the question, Apple said, "No, sir. You're pacing it nicely."

"Your cover is that you are the child of people in the theatrical business. You were raised by your parents while they were travelling around Europe. You, like all such people, speak half-a-dozen languages. *But not well.* Remember that, please. Don't suddenly get fluent in anything."

"No, sir."

"Your story is that you miss the old life. You crave the company and talk of people who are still in it. A cover that's nice

and simple. You need to do no research. It's eminently fake-
able."

"I am a fan of the theatre, as it happens, sir," Apple said,
pleased to be telling the truth. Because of this, he repeated his
statement, reversing the sentence.

Watkin bored on, "You will be given the keys to a suitable
car. In it will be a change of clothes which were taken from your
flat an hour ago. You will be given money. Last of all, you will
be given your ticket. It's for this evening's performance. You
ought to get there in time, if you don't dawdle."

"Ticket?" Apple said obligingly. "Performance?" He could
sense that his superior was about to make himself happy with
another surprise.

"You are going," Angus Watkin said, "to a circus."

The countryside and byways were pretty, the villages were
quaint. This was felt rather than seen, for Apple was too full of
himself to pay close attention. He was also driving too fast to
take in details.

Apple sat leaning forward, gripping the wheel hard. Some cars
he passed on the inside, others he cut around like a teenager
with his first jalopy. He had broken the speed laws a dozen
times before finally leaving London behind and continued doing
so in every built-up area. He snarled at delays and saw every
traffic light as green. Never had he driven so badly.

The car, as Watkin had said, was suitable. What else would a
market gardener have but a battered station wagon? Furthermore, the Ford had soil and leaves strewn around in the back,
plus a couple of seed boxes.

Apple was in similar character. Before leaving the garage, he
had changed into jeans, an open-neck shirt, and a windcheater

in brown leather. His jeans being clean, he had rubbed dirt over the knees. He had scuffled his hair to a nice untidiness.

Apple was happy: with his appearance, with the rakish car, and most of all with the mission—the fact of being on one, rather than the job itself. It seemed formless, for one thing. For another, he had a niggle of doubt about the long-term effect of the drug, which had been given the code-name of Soma-2. But Apple was happy. Even when he snarled, slowed behind a lumbering truck, he was enjoying himself.

The destination was Taunton, in Somerset. Pitched outside the town were the tent and trucks and trailers of Sir Jasper Ranklin's International Circus, along with the usual accompanying fairground rides and attractions.

Sir Jasper was a Yorkshireman, Apple had learned over tea at the garage, a plain lad of the woollen mills who had risen to own a mill of his own. He had been knighted for his efforts in the export trade that had made him wealthy. At sixty, five years ago, he had realized a life-long ambition. He had joined a circus —his own. It was his toy. He was boss and ringmaster and worried not at all that, in this age of television, he was losing a thousand pounds a week. Apple understood perfectly.

There were twelve acts, all billed as foreign, though some were no more alien to the British Isles than fish and chips. Among the genuine there were a Chinese group, jugglers; French acrobats; German aerialists; a Spanish contortionist; two Italian escape artists; a Finnish strong-man; a Hungarian animal act.

It was the last that Apple would give his attention to: Tina Koves and her Wild Gorillas. Tina had a partner/manager/ring assistant by the name of Anton Gavor. A third, dim member of the troupe, Tibor Polk, took care of the animals.

Anton Gavor it was, at Sir Jasper's birthday party, who had

brought in his pop bottle and made the evening into a riotous success.

Apple raced along a village street. An old man shook his cane in anger, a dog got out of the way in time, a child yelled with fear. Though Apple mumbled an excuse me, it was only automatic.

His thoughts were on the person who had lifted the bottle, taken Soma-2 while the truth game was going on. Watkin had admitted, with reluctance, that the lifter was an operative, with the circus to keep an eye on the Chinese, whose claim to being from Taiwan seemed a little frail.

"How do I contact him?" Apple had asked.

"You do not, Porter. Under any circumstances. But, of course, you don't know the person's identity. I'm not going to tell you, and don't you try to find out. That's another kettle of fish altogether. Stay clear of it."

"Yes, sir." He had made note of the fact that Watkin had not stated any gender.

Swerving around corners, Apple had a romantic vision of the Chinese-watcher turning out to be a beautiful girl, of her falling in love with him and him with her, of her being revealed as a double-spy. For a while, it kept him off the subject of the drug.

As in the world of sport, the use of narcotics is widespread in animal training and performing, though equally illegal whether administered to a miler or a lion. But where in sport the illegality is toward the various associations, all civil, in the animal field it is in respect of the nation's criminal code. Banned from a track-meet for one, a possibility of prison for the other.

"Okay for people," Apple said to the road, "but don't fool around with animals. What a country."

Soma-2 was probably being used on the gorillas in Tina's act, Watkin had said, for the big apes were notoriously the least tameable and friendly of all the simians. With his drug, Anton Gavor would be able to keep them as willing to please as a man being interrogated.

But Anton wouldn't want anyone to know about it, Apple thought, not even the people he worked among. Perhaps, taking that to the extreme, even the woman who made the animals perform. It wasn't being romantic to think there could be a situation where the man loved the woman and wanted to make her believe she was a genius with animals.

Which, Apple mused with satisfaction, would make the mission much more difficult. A man might own up to using a drug to further the cause of entertainment, but never if it were in the convolutions of love.

Apple was further pleased to realize that, at the circus, he would be able to look over the girl who had told those devastating truths. He would soon be able to tell if her health was holding up.

A signpost said that Taunton was two miles. Apple slowed the station wagon. When he came among houses he crawled until he saw a child, having passed several adults, stopped and asked the way to the circus field. Told eagerly, in a jabber, he blew the little girl a kiss and drove on.

He remembered that this was the show's second day in the region, that the week before it had been in Dorchester, that in five days it would move on elsewhere. It occurred to him that, although it could be fun to spend the summer moving around with a circus, if he didn't wrap up his mission with dispatch he might never get a chance at another.

Apple broke the speed laws again to cut through suburbs. He came out onto the Bridgwater Road and turned away from town. In a minute he was close. A field on the left was full of parked cars, the one right was a jumble of colour around a high-swooping dome of grey canvas. Stretched between the tent's main poles was a banner. It said SIR JASPER RANKLIN'S IN-TERNATIONAL CIRCUS.

"What time does the show start?"

"In fifteen minutes. You got plenty of time, sport. Now what d'you say? Three balls for fifty pence."

"I suppose you know all the people in the show, don't you?"

"Me, I never bother with circus folk. They're odd."

"I've always thought them very sane," Apple said. He was standing at the counter of a coconut shy. It was the first stall at one side of the broad avenue, which was lined with entertainments and which led, from the field's gate, to the canopied entrance of the big top.

"I'll tell you what I'm gonna do," the coconut shy man said. "I'm gonna make it four balls for the price of three." He put on a face of shock at his generosity.

"Later," Apple said. "I promise." He moved away. Instead of going on up the avenue, he went around the back. Living trailers and trucks were jumbled together thickly, close to the tent. Apple went forward. He entered the pack of vehicles.

After circling trucks, he passed around a trailer, and gasped at the deep growl that erupted beside him. Lion, he told himself as he stepped quickly away; then, elephant, as the growl rose to a shrill trumpeting.

Into view came a man. In a red uniform with gold trimmings, he was carrying a trombone. He put it to his lips and started on another growl. With the pitch rising, he went on walking amongst the equipment.

Heart slowing to normal, Apple followed.

He was led to what constituted backstage: a large lean-to tent on the side of the big one. It had flaps open in a number of places. Inside, where the trombonist had gone, were scores of people. Some were in band uniform, some wore the simple blue tunics of attendants, some had on the customary spangles and tights, some were in overalls. There was a steady boom of noise —talk, laughter, shouted orders, the musicians' practice trills.

Cautiously, Apple went closer to a flap. Peering through, he concentrated on isolating the artistes. The Chinese were easy, a group of four youngish men. He also picked out the Germans, on account of their dress; strong-man Finn in a leopard skin; and the Italian escape artists, who were untangling a pile of chains.

Near the flap, a patch of clowns was huddled over an argument. The subject was football, with the accents ranging from Scots to Swedish. The loudest, most abusive arguer was a man in white-face, red nose, and shaggy wig of bright orange. He wore a one-piece suit in black and white checks.

It wasn't manner that made Apple notice this clown, it was shape. If not quite as tall as Apple, he was a great deal thinner. He towered skinnily over the others, including two dwarves, and berated their teams in a Glasgow accent.

As though sensing Apple's attention, the clown turned his head. Briefly, between the two tall men flashed a look of understanding. Apple smiled and nodded. Not responding in kind, the clown left the others and came over.

Without emotion he asked, "Looking for something?"

"Nothing in particular," Apple said.

"You don't have to pretend. But she isn't here."

"Who isn't here?"

"Tina Koves."

Apple was still in his surprise at being given one of the important names of his mission, when the clown added, "We get all the stage-door romeos sniffing around here after Tina. Don't waste your time."

Apple put on disappointment. "Why not?"

The clown adjusted his wig as if it were a beret. "Because. That's why." His eyes flicked beyond Apple. "Or you could try asking her ape-keeper, old Tibor. There he goes. But don't hang around here."

He and Apple turned away from each other at the same time. Apple saw, crossing a stretch of grass between trucks, a small man of about fifty. He wore a soiled green smock. His hair was grey at the sides, white on top. He had a mournful expression.

Tibor Polk went from sight. Apple hurried to follow. Thinking to make a short cut, he took another, indirect route, along beside a storage trailer. Around its farther end, he found no sign of the Hungarian. He still didn't see him after going down several of the mazelike alleys of grass between vehicles. Giving up, he even had trouble finding his way back to the open.

Apple returned to the midway avenue. Thousands of light bulbs glowed against the first hint of evening. People streamed past toward the tent entrance, where a man was beating out ponderous booms on a bass drum.

Going the same way, Apple passed ball games, a dart stall, dive-bomber, a helter skelter, and a Wall of Death where two youths were revving up their raucous motorcycles. Among the people and the racket, the blare of music and the insistent drum, Apple began to feel excited. He told himself it was the mission.

From a day of soaking up sun, the tent was warm. It smelt exactly the way it should; a bouquet formed of sawdust and animals and grass, sugar and popcorn and greasepaint. The lights were party bright, as was the atmosphere. The band was ripping and stomping through a march that was a tenting show tradition.

Sitting on his numbered section of plank seat, three rows from the rim of the ring, Apple looked around. He was comforted by the number of adults among the children, with a particularly heavy sprinkling of men; comforted both for the acceptableness of his own presence, and because it showed there was still interest in the old-fashioned entertainments. From a youth with a tray, he bought a bag of popcorn.

Over the next hour, until interval, Apple remembered the mission only intermittently. He was fascinated by the horse act and the jugglers, amazed by the Finn's strength, and scared sweaty by the German trapeze artists. He knew the escapists would never get out of their chains and straight jackets, and applauded limp from tension when they did. At the antics of the clowns, he laughed almost to the point of embarrassment; the skinny Scot, announced as Nick Stick, was funnier than Apple would ever have guessed.

Announcing was done by the ringmaster. Sir Jasper Ranklin used a megaphone. A short, stout man with a cherubic face, he wore top hat and tails. Flushed, eyes bright, he looked to be having the time of his life.

During intermission, the blue-clad attendants carried in sections of iron grillwork, each a yard wide and three yards tall. A square cage was built. It had a top as well as sides. Other sections of bars were used to create a low tunnel; it led from the cage to the depths of backstage.

When the job was finished, a man entered the ring. He had on a tight-fitting uniform jacket, riding britches, and boots. His head was shaven. Aged about thirty-five, he had the brisk, cool manner of a professional soldier. Apple knew he was looking at Anton Gavor.

34

The Hungarian circled the cage, checking bolts. He had a strong, square jaw and a nose as blunt as a knee. His black eyes were set close together. All in all, the face was perfectly suited to the bullet head and clothing—smooth and hard, even ruthless.

Checking over, Anton Gavor strolled out of the ring.

The band blared in fanfare. The interval lights lowered and Sir Jasper appeared in a spotlight. He raised his megaphone. Turning the while, he called out in ringing, lingering tones:

"My lords, ladies and gentlemen. Preee-senting. One of the most sensational acts ever seen, anytime, anywhere. Five wild, feee-rocious, uncontrollable, and unpredictable beasts of the jungle. Savage. Brutal. Cunning. Of inhuman strength. Tonight you will . . ."

Along the tunnel, on all-fours, came the gorillas. They were huge. They filled the yard-square space, their shoulders and backs raising a clatter as they brushed along the bars. They had the faces of evil old men.

Once in the cage, the animals stood stoopingly erect. One made the audience gasp; first by leaping up onto the top grillwork, next by shaking the cage so that it looked and sounded to be on the point of falling apart. The other four gorillas grabbed bars, glared through and bared their fangs.

". . . weighing more than two hundred and fifty pounds apiece," Sir Jasper was saying. "And who will work with these raging monster apes? Ten strong men? A robot in a tank? No, my friends, only the courageous, brilliant, beautiful daughter of the Hungarian mountains. The one, the unique—Tina Koves!"

Applause started and swelled. The spotlight moved. It picked up a figure coming from backstage: an unusually small figure. Apple craned his neck for a better view.

Tina was not much over five feet tall. Dusky blond hair was drawn back into a clasp, from where it fell in a tail to beyond her waist. From head to toe she was naked except for the skimp-iest of bikinis, made of white silk. Her body, slender but volup-tuously formed, gleamed with oil. Her face had classical fea-tures. Tina Koves was ragingly attractive.

She entered the cage and sauntered to its centre. Bearing neither rod nor whip, she put her hands elegantly on her hips, which she began to sway. She kept time with the music. It was a slow and sensuous murmur with a jungle-drum suggestion.

In the penumbra of the lights that shone down into the cage, a shape moved. Reluctantly, Apple took his eyes off the girl. The shape was Anton Gavor. He carried a rifle. Apple doubted if it was loaded, but he appreciated the showmanship. He gave his avid attention back to the act.

It made him tense, despite his knowing that there was proba-bly little danger. It stirred him, though he could see that there was almost no skill or talent involved. Mainly, it affected him sensually.

The animal act was decidedly erotic. Apple understood now the clown's talk of stage-door romeos as well as why there were so many men in the audience.

Moving slowly to the music, Tina Koves performed a strolling semi-dance in her work with the gorillas. She stood on their chests as they lay supine, swung over their backs as they crouched. Her body glistening, she stroked their shoulders, slipped in and out of their embraces, led them on an amble around the cage. She used only her voice to get obedience.

The gorillas themselves did little apart from looking wild. They didn't appear to be doped. They snarled, swayed, reached out long arms toward the girl. They could attack her at any second, it seemed, and were held back from doing so only by her words.

There were none of the tricks common to animal acts, those

caperings which Apple sometimes found offensive. Now he didn't even add to his enjoyment by noting their absence. He was captivated by the image of slim, young femininity, virginal in token white, playing temptress to gross caricatures of the brute, lusting male.

There was no finale, as such; no thrust of action. With the music fading, Tina took the face of each gorilla in turn between her hands, moved on sadly, at last backed away as if sorry to leave—and slipped out of the cage. The ring went dark.

Although the applause was light at first, hesitant, it swiftly grew in volume. Apple joined it but at a plod. He felt depleted. Tina Koves's act had been the last straw in an eventful, nerve-shaking day.

Apple got up and sidled to the aisle. It was time to go and find a hotel.

CHAPTER 2

Wintertree catered mostly to commercial travellers. They were lying to each other about sales when Apple came into the lobby the next morning, after just making the last call for breakfast. He had missed not having his lemon marmalade to go with the toast.

By way of beckon, the proprietress leaned at him from over the reception desk. She was a sturdy matron with eyes that missed nothing. Apple went across.

"Will you be staying a second night, sir?"

"Yes," he said. "Maybe more." For practice, he told his cover story. It sounded not only straightforward, but engaging. "The Amazing Porters. You may have heard of them. Tightrope walkers."

The woman, looking impressed, shook her head. "My Jimmy might have heard. He's mad about show biz. Collects souvenirs and autographs. I'll ask him, if you like."

Apple said it didn't matter. He went out to the suburban street—and into another fine day. Getting in the station wagon, which surprised him by starting on the first buzz, he made a U-turn and headed out of town. He should not, he told himself, have been surprised. The motor was probably tuned within an inch of its life. There could even be a supercharger hidden somewhere.

Apple drove on. He tried to recall the dirtier bits of last

night's dream about Tina Koves, until he reached the parking field. It was empty. He left the car there and went across to the other side.

The shows were still shrouded from their overnight rest, though some operators were in attendance on various tasks. From one, Apple got the location of Sir Jasper's trailer. He was going to do this the polite way, which meant the clever way.

The Ranklin mobile home was high, square, and old-fashioned, as Apple might have expected. It was parked amid the general jumble of vehicles. Sir Jasper, attended by a manservant, sat having breakfast at a table on the grass. He wore a braided dressing gown.

Approaching, Apple said, "Good morning. May I introduce myself?"

The knight changed his welcome from mild to affable when he heard about the Amazing Porters. "Sit down, lad," he said. "Had brekker? Then have some coffee. Look sharp, Marton. So, lad, you're a child of the big top, eh?"

Apple had no need to be inventive. He didn't get the chance to try. Sir Jasper rolled the conversational ball nimbly and firmly, passing it across out of politeness once in a while, but retrieving at practiced speed. He talked of the circus world, from Ancient Rome's Maximus on to the present day.

Apple heard, and stored for his own possible use, about Lord John Sanger, Bertram-Mills, Billy Smart, the Chipperfields; about the tent fire in Hartford, Connecticut; about Barnum, Bailey, Colonel North, the Ringling Brothers.

At last, after two coffees served by the silent Marton, Apple got up to leave. He said, "I hope you won't mind, sir, if I nose about the circus a bit, while I'm in the area. It's like being back home again."

"I met him for the first time today," Apple said. Again, he gave his cover story. He was pleased to realize that he was beginning to believe it—the mark of a pro.

Nick Stick relaxed in body and skeletal face. He started to talk about his own life as a circus brat.

When they got out of the car, it was a natural move to go in the pub together and stay that way at the bar. The clown waved at several people, one a dwarf, and told the barmaid, "Two pints, please." He paid. They took their glasses out to the garden, where they sat among other customers on rusty furniture.

They sipped beer, lit cigarettes. Apple said, "Sir Jasper mentioned his birthday party. Sounds as if it was quite a bash. Pity I hadn't been in Dorchester last week."

Nick Stick grinned. "Funniest bloody thing I ever heard."

"I believe someone did fantastic card tricks."

"Sure, but there was this girl that Anton hypnotised. I tell you, I was in stitches."

Apple persisted cleverly, "I can never figure out how they do those tricks with cards, can you?"

He had out-clevered himself. The clown, nodding, started on an explanation of the basic card trick, to which Apple didn't listen. He consoled himself by getting rid of some of his beer, holding the glass down at his side and tilting it gently.

Nick Stick asked, "You see what I mean?"

"No, it's beyond me. Don't bother." He sipped. "How long have you been with this outfit?"

"Five or six weeks, same as most of the artistes. The show's been off the road all winter, of course."

"And there's the usual easy fellowship, I suppose, in spite of the different nationalities. I spoke to the Hungarians earlier. They were very friendly."

Nick Stick gave a humourless laugh. "That's only on the surface. They never go further than that. Stuck-up lot. Think they've got the best act in the world and everyone else should go and perform in the street."

"But didn't you just say that Anton joined in at the party?"

The clown gave his slanting, weighing nod. "Funny that. He seemed to blossom, for some reason or another. He was back to normal next day."

"Hypnosis, did you say?"

Grinning, the clown told about the truth-telling session. All Apple learned, above what he had been given by Angus Watkin, was the nature of the slanders.

"Me, Mavis said I was like something a dog had buried. She said she was sick of Antonio trying to grope her in corners—Antonio's wife loved that, you can be sure. She said the Chinese boys were a bunch of Commie spies." He listed others. "And I'd hate to tell you Mavis's opinion of the boss. Poor old fella. He was livid. I'm surprised he told you about it."

"He didn't. Not about that. Only the pleasant bits."

"Believe me, it was hi-larious."

Apple supplied cigarettes and a light. "Has the girl lived it down yet, or is she still suffering?"

"Search me," Nick Stick said. He blew out a long thin stream of smoke. "The boss let her go a couple of days later. Can't blame him. She was only programme-popcorn-tickets. Replaceable as a hangover. These kids practically beg to be taken on in the thrilling, romantic, glamorous life of the big top."

Apple said, "Still, poor Mavis. I hope she had enough money to get back to her home town—wherever that was."

"So do I."

"She may have lived at the other end of the country."

"Never know," the clown said. He drained his glass. "Come

on, we'll have another at the bar before I get back to thrills, romance, and glamour."

Coming out of the restaurant, Apple belched. He felt queasy: the one and a half pints of beer he had been unable to get out of drinking, the meal he had just forced himself to eat in order to sop up the beer. It had taken forever for the lamb curry to be served, and he knew it would take longer for it to be digested. He belched again. There was no one near.

Gradually, as Apple wandered on a window-shop around the centre of Taunton, he began to feel better in body. His spirits took a matching rise. He had had an interesting talk with Nick Stick, with whom he was now on first-name terms, and who, with Sir Jasper, formed another close ally at the circus. A third, Apple reminded himself, could be made with no trouble at all.

He went back to his car and drove out of town.

Now the field used as a parking area was filling. Apple left the station wagon there and went across the road. It pleased him to be remembered by the coconut shy man, who said:

"Good day to you, sport."

"Hello," Apple said. "I promised to come back and have a go, and here I am."

The man laughed. He was grizzled, roughly dressed but wearing a gleamingly new straw hat. "Don't worry about that," he said. "The word's gone 'round. You're one of us."

"I told you that yesterday."

"People're always claiming the same thing. They think they can get free rides and nick in to see the show for nothing. Of course, if they're genuine, they *can*."

"Even so," Apple said, "I insist on having a go and paying for it." He put down a coin. "Four balls, I believe you offered."

The man laughed indulgently. "Take five. But if you win a

nut, I'll buy it back from you, if you don't mind. They're a bit scarce this summer."

Between the throwing of each ball, missing every time, Apple asked a question. What did the man think of this one, that one? He learned nothing of value.

Strolling on among the crowd, Apple found himself exchanging friendly nods with stall-holders. A woman at the candy floss stand offered him a free helping of the pink fluff. He declined with thanks, fighting a belch. The word, he thought, had gone around with a vengeance.

Joining a semicircle of audience, Apple watched the dive-bomber. This ride was two cigar-shaped cockpits, one at either end of a heavy bar, the middle of which was balanced on top of a pylon. The cockpits twirled on the bar while the bar twirled and dipped on its axis.

The ride was in action. Although none of the movements were overly fast, the occupants, female, were shrieking, especially as the glass-nosed cockpits came down, when the girls' dresses lifted above their waists. Apple watched with scientific interest.

The ride slowed, ended. Apple was on the point of drifting away when the owner approached him. She was a tall woman dressed to look like an old-fashioned pilot, an Amelia Earhart, in boots and leathers and flying helmet. The goggles were down over her eyes.

"Hello there," she said boisterously, causing other drifters to pause. "If you'd care to take a turn, it's on the house."

Apple smilingly shook his head. "No, thank you."

Joshingly: "Oh, come on. You'll enjoy it."

"You're very kind, but I think I'm a bit too old for that kind of thing. Also I'm on the tall side."

"I've seen bigger than you get in there."

48

A man from the audience called out, "Have a bash." A girl said, "He's scared."

Amelia Earhart took his arm. "There's nothing to be scared of. Kids go on it all the time."

"Oh well," Apple said, feeling abused. "Why not?"

He let himself be led to the cockpit that was down at ground level; its twin was perched high aloft at the bar's other end. He squeezed in. His head was an inch from the Plexiglas top. Amelia Earhart buckled a strap tightly around his middle, stepped back and slammed the door, winked, and went to a nearby control box.

The cockpit started to move. Slowly it rose. Apple expected it to stop at the top, in order for the twin to take on a passenger, but there was no stopping. The speed increased.

Apple held on to the handle at either side. The cockpit began to turn. He went upside down, and the top of his head hit the roof. Next, he was being dropped back into the seat. He saw flashes of earth and sky and people.

The speed increased still more. From all the pressures on his body, Apple knew suddenly that this couldn't be normal. No child could take it, no adult would stand for it without complaining afterwards. Apple felt the assault of fear.

The changes of scene became flicks across his vision. Rapidly he was being jerked from side to side, as well as up and down. His arms thudded against the sides, his head and buttocks were repeatedly battered. He went around and around, spun over and over.

Voices rose in a jabber. They had a quality of alarm.

The speed grew. Vision was a continual blur without divisions. Apple felt he couldn't stand the pressures and bashings for another second. His nose seemed to be bleeding.

One voice rose above the others, calling, "It's out of control!"

Abruptly, Apple's queasiness of stomach returned. He tasted bile. The nausea filled him inside as completely as the pain was bathing the exterior. He was going to vomit. Now. A splurge was rising.

"Stop it!" voices shouted. They came to Apple's dazed hearing as if from far away. "Somebody stop it!" He begged the same in his mind—and wondered if screaming the plea would help.

Apple began to lose consciousness. He closed his eyes against the visual blur. As his body relaxed, the batterings increased. Time after time his head thumped against the roof. His hands, wrenched with pain from gripping so hard, began to slip away from the handles.

Next Apple knew, it was all over. The slowing had been rapid, and the stop fast. He opened his eyes to find the owner staring at him anxiously while unfastening the strap. There was an excited buzz of talk in the background.

"You all right?" Amelia Earhart asked. "You okay?"

Lying insanely with limp nods, Apple got himself out, helped by the woman, who kept saying, "I don't know what happened. Sure you're feeling all right? You look terrible."

Apple couldn't speak. The vomit was choking him in its struggle for instant release. Fear gone, pride made him hold on. He nodded again, eased himself free of the woman's solicitous hands, turned away from the crowd. Dizzy, he went into the maze at a weaving walk.

Apple threw up near a collection of garbage bags. The sight of one of these, split, settled his indecision over whether or not to give in. Throat tearing, he retched until cleansed of the nausea. After kicking soil over the mess, he moved weakly to the closest vehicle, a high-sitting truck-trailer. He crawled under it and sprawled out on his back. It felt good to be alive.

Presently, Apple thought about the dive-bomber. Its speed, of course, could have been a mistake. Something wrong with the controls. But he hoped it had been deliberate. That would be a good sign.

Apple dozed off.

He awoke to find a face peering at him. The face was upside down. Hair dangled from it like a straggly beard. Out of the mouth at the top came the voice of a young boy. It said, "There you are."

"So it would seem."

"I been looking all over for you, Mr. Porter. What you doing?"

"My father used to have a truck-trailer like this," Apple said. He looked away from the weirdness of the inverse face. "I used to play under it as a kid."

"Well, never mind," the boy said. "The thing is, Sir Jasper told me to tell you that you're invited to drinks tonight at his wagon, after the show."

"Thank you. Please tell Sir Jasper that I accept, with pleasure."

"See, there'll be someone there who might've known your parents, he said to tell you. Okay?"

"Okay."

The boy went. Apple, drinks in mind, wondered if his being nauseated was due to the beer. Or could it be the beginnings of a possible long-term effect of Soma-2? Or was it only sheer funk?

He dozed again.

The chill of late afternoon brought him awake. He sighed, yawned, and brought up both hands to rub his face. The left hand, he found, wasn't empty. He was holding a piece of paper, folded small. Crawling out into the open, he got to his feet. He unfolded the paper. On it was written GO AWAY.

Apple didn't know whether to laugh or to be impressed. He chose the latter, after looking at the message with care for a minute. Obviously, he had touched someone on a raw spot. That's the reason he was here. The note meant he was making progress.

Putting the paper in his pocket, Apple went cheerfully in search of water. He found a tap and rinsed out his mouth, next washed his face. For a towel he used the front of his pulled-up shirt. Tidy again, he went on. He knew the way now.

One of the matching pair of grey trailers had an awning out front. It was in red and white stripes and had a pretty fringe. Apple went underneath, where he had to crouch until he got right beside the trailer, near the door, on which it said that this was the home of Tina Koves and that visitors were not allowed.

Apple knocked. After a short pause, the door swung out. The trailer floor being about two feet above the ground, Tina Koves was on eye level with Apple. He didn't know if it was that fact or his presence that caused her to frown along with a curt:

"You did not read the sign."

He answered in Magyar, "Yes, I did, but I thought you wouldn't mind. I wanted to tell you how much I enjoyed your show last night."

"Thank you," Tina said, staying with English. Apple decided to go along with her on the language question. He had been through this before.

He said, "I've seen a lot of animal acts in my life, but yours is the most sensational. You may have heard that I'm from a theatrical family."

Tina nodded. If such a thing were possible, she was more attractive now than when she had been performing. She wore a white shirt, open almost to the navel, with no material crossing the gap to suggest the presence of a bra. Her hair was in two braids; they trailed down on the outsides of her pert breasts. The hem of the tight, white skirt lay at mid-thigh. Again, she was barefooted. To the voluptuous body had been added a suggestion of little-girl innocence.

"My name is Appleton Porter. Friends call me Apple."

"How curious," Tina said. She reached forward to get the door, thereby showing the inner curves of her breasts. "What an odd name."

Apple squeezed gently at the door he was holding fully back, out of easy reach. "Your name is sweet, Tina. I hope you don't mind me calling you that. After all, we are colleagues, in a way, and I do speak Hungarian, which is the most beautiful of all languages."

Tina had leaned back again. "Yes," she said mildly, "you are right."

"My parents often performed in Hungary, with their animal act. It was a good act, but, frankly, it was nothing compared to yours. Your control over the gorillas is nothing short of fantastic."

"Many thanks. What you say is true."

"Did you train them with kindness or the whip?"

"The door, please."

"What?"

"Would you swing the door to me," Tina Koves said. "I have to close it."

Apple asked a winning, "Why right now?"

"Because I have to get undressed and I cannot do so with the door open. Nor can I ask you in because I do not know you well enough to get undressed in front of you."

"I could keep my eyes closed."

"That," Tina said, "would not be very exciting." She gestured. "The door, if you would be so kind."

Apple brought it to the right-angle position. "May I come and talk to you again, Tina?"

She said an enigmatic, "That remains to be seen." Leaning forward, further than before, she managed to make contact with the handle. A good portion of inner bosom displayed itself tremblingly.

"Thank you," Apple said. "I'll come this evening or tomorrow morning."

"Or the day after. Or the day after that." She drew the door closed on a cool, "Good afternoon."

Sighing, Apple moved out from under the awning. Tina Koves, he mused, was the sexiest creature he had ever met. He smiled sadly on recalling his daydream, for Tina could never fulfill the role of the Chinese-watcher, who was probably someone of the ilk of Nick Stick.

From the other trailer, Tibor Polk appeared. He was carrying a water-jack. Turning the other way, head down, he moved off between vehicles. Apple followed, but slowly.

By the time he had caught up, was walking sociably beside the older man, Apple had come to the conclusion that he was possibly pushing too hard on the animal theme. It had, in any case, an instant cooling effect. Which was understandable. Not only did the troupe, or Anton alone, have prosecution to fear from someone who could be an RSPCA snooper, there was loss of livelihood—the act being banned—or at least the secret being stolen by a competitor. The act would be gravely reduced if there were dozens of others like it.

So while Apple accompanied Tibor Polk to the tap, while the can filled, and while Apple did the return carrying, he spoke only of general matters. He earned a good response. Tibor even smiled once, and he was effusive in his thanks for the help when they reached the trailer.

"My pleasure," Apple said. "But, as a matter of fact, I would appreciate a little help myself."

"Which would be?"

"I'd like to talk to Anton. A private matter. Would you, perhaps, ask him if he could spare me ten minutes sometime?"

Tibor ran a hand over his white hair. "Anton is not a sociable man. But yes, I will ask."

At Wintertree, Apple was delayed by the landlady's son. Jimmy, a gangly youth with his upper front teeth missing, wanted an autograph as well as the whole history of the Amazing Porters. Apple fobbed him with a signature scribbled in a book the size of a telephone directory.

Not until he was getting out of his clothes did Apple feel the results of his dive-bomber ride. One muscle seemed to tell another, which passed it on. By the time he was lowering himself into the steaming bath, he was a mass of aches. From Training Six he recalled the advice, *To hold off after-effects, keep the game rolling.* The game, for now, was being played in the lockerroom. As far as Apple was concerned, reality was the wet heat that kneaded and caressed his body gently.

He extended that reality for an hour, with frequent additions from the hot tap. Finishing with a cold shower, he patted himself dry, not up to a brisk rub even though most of his aches had gone. The remainder were mild. Only the top of his head and the base of his spine told him that his experience had been out of the ordinary. He felt generally fine, and hungry.

Dressed in suit, shirt, and tie, Apple went downstairs and allowed himself to be waylaid by Jimmy, to whom he lied elaborately and with exciting detail for a quarter hour. Next, thinking warmly of his kindness, he went to find a restaurant.

Walking, Apple was assuring himself that a market gardener would own at least one respectable suit, when it occurred to him that he need not have dressed in his own everyday clothes. He could have bought—could still buy—something else. There was a legitimate reason, and the cost would go on expenses. Furthermore, since there was little use the Service would have for clothing to fit a man his size, he would be told to keep it.

In defence of this outrageous idea, which almost made him blush, Apple argued that all he was doing was acting like a pro, being a padder or thinking to be. If he couldn't function like one, he might never be one.

Apple recalled the recent case of the operative who, to bring out a neighbour on whom the Service had its eye, had started to have a swimming pool built in his garden. It was nearly finished by the time the neighbour turned out to be innocent. The pool-owning agent was still active, even though it had been definitely proved that the tip on his neighbour had come from him in the first place.

So it didn't matter, Apple thought. But he was relieved to realize that the stores were all long since closed. And now he was able to remind himself that he had no need of padding. He was reasonably off. He got a retainer from the Service in addition to his excellent wage from the United Kingdom Philological Institute.

The restaurant was small and select. Out of shame, Apple settled only on items that were no more expensive than those he would usually choose. With his coffee he had a Spanish *coñac* of a brand he hated, which he never touched, but which was cheaper than the others. He didn't drink it.

Driving out of town, Apple met a heavy flow of traffic going in the opposite direction. The evening performance, he realized, had ended. He wondered how many of those drivers would go to bed hoping to dream of Tina Koves; and, smugly, how much they would give to get as close to her as he had been.

There were still plenty of cars in the parking field, for the fairground attractions, when Apple drove in. He parked, locked up the station wagon securely and went over into the glare of moving and blinking lights.

The coconut shy was busy, as were the other stalls. At the dive-bomber, Apple had to wait ten minutes before he could get Amelia Earhart to himself. She looked subdued behind her goggles.

"I can't understand it," she said after apologising again. "I don't know what could have gone wrong with those controls."

"You'd better have them checked."

"I have. Real thorough. They're perfect."

Apple said, laughing, "If I'd been killed, it might have looked curious—the way you insisted on me having a ride."

The woman looked shocked. "But I thought you'd understand, you being one of us. I only wanted to keep the joint busy. It makes for more trade."

Which, Apple thought as he moved on a minute later, could well be true. It could also be true that, while the uptempo had been deliberate, it had been so with a nonsinister motive: someone who, assuming Apple to be used to such rides, wanted to give him a better trip than he would get from a cautious woman. But Apple didn't believe that.

"It's the cost of living, old man."

"Inflation, you mean. That is where the problem lies."

"I told Hans, we must get this child braces for her teeth."

"She will tank you for dat later in life, but not now."

"Those old curtains were a mess, my dear, so what I did was, I buy myself some new pieces for the edges."

"How very clever of you, Mrs. Carletti."

Apple was amused, as well as slightly depressed, to realize that a cocktail party at a circus was no different from one anywhere else, except for the broken accents. The conversation and attitudes were the same, as were the drinks and canapés—these being served by Sir Jasper Ranklin's manservant.

Twelve people were crowded into the lounge end of the big living wagon, which was quietly luxurious. The walls were panelled in teak, the floor spread with Persian rugs. Lighting came courtesy of a chandelier. For decoration there were framed miniatures of old-time circus posters, one featuring Houdini.

The guests were two of the German aerialists with their wives; the Finn, a huge man with long hair and a beard; Tina and Anton; one of the Chinese juggling quartet; half of the Italian escape artist team, plus his wife.

The uninvited would not feel left out, Apple had already learned, for these affairs were a regular feature of the Ranklin show. Everyone had a turn.

This Apple had been told by one of the German women, a large blonde. She spoke English with a perfection and precision that no Britisher would dare attempt, for fear of sounding ridiculous. Apple hoped his German had a more natural resonance.

"Sir Jasper does seem remarkably fond of parties," he said. "I've heard about that one in Dorchester."

The blonde frowned. "It was painful. An embarrassment for everybody. I personally did not consider it to be at all edifying or entertaining."

"I don't suppose Mavis Jones does, either."

"Regland. Mavis Regland. The poor thing."

"Yes," Apple said. "Lost her job and had to go all the way back to Manchester."

"Chepton Vale, near Bath. I do hope her parents will take an understanding attitude."

Anton Gavor stepped forward to make up a third side. "Understanding? Yes, quite so. That is what the whole world needs, is it not?" The light shone on his shaven head like sun on an apple.

The woman's body stiffened, though her face stayed pleasant. "The world," she said, "needs a great number of things."

"They can all be taken care of under the umbrella of understanding," Anton said. "You must agree."

"There is nothing I *must* do, Mr. Gavor."

Apple left them to it and sidled away. This wasn't the moment to try for a talk with the Hungarian. Besides, Tina was at the farther end of the lounge.

For the next half hour, nursing his drink, Apple tried to get close to where Tina was being monopolised by the Italian and the strong-man. He was stopped first by the former's wife, who told him about her curtains, next by Sir Jasper, who wanted to boast about his poster miniatures.

Tina wore what seemed to be her favourite shade—white. Apart from that, the dress was the "simple little" that every woman had in her wardrobe for cocktail parties. On Tina it looked little but not simple. Her hair was still dressed for the show, in a pony-tail. She was taller, almost average height, in high-heel shoes.

Every time his glance had caught Tina's, Apple had smiled, but without getting a like return. At last, now, she began to smile back. Apple wondered if it had anything to do with the fact that she was repeatedly getting fresh drinks—straight whisky.

Sir Jasper said, "But enough of this, lad. You have to talk to Arvo. Come along."

They went to the trio at the end, who were diplomatic about letting the boss interrupt their talk. He said, "Arvo, it's possible you knew Mr. Porter's parents years ago."

Apple had already been introduced to the Finn, along with the other guests, when he had arrived. The strong-man looked woefully out of place in a lounge suit, like a lumberjack at a wedding. After confessing that he never remembered the names of acts, he began to ask questions about various Continental tenting shows.

Apple did well. In the approved manner of Training Four, he used more attack than defence. He asked, "Are you sure you have the year right?" or, "Wasn't that Berlin, not Frankfurt?" or, "Could the Royal Dutch Circus have been there at that time?" The Finn, drinking vodka steadily, seemed not to care.

Tina told him, "But listen, even without the name, you surely can remember an English couple wfth animals?"

The other guests had been talking less. They stopped altogether as Sir Jasper said loudly, "Animals? But you told me, lad, that your folk were acrobats."

Apple was pleased to find himself staying cool, in spite of the charge and of being the centre of acute attention. The reason for this was, he felt clever. At once he had found not only the answer, but a peg to hang his briefcase on.

"Yes, I did tell you that," he said easily. "I always do. My parents did perform tumbles during their act with the bears, so I call them acrobats, not mentioning the animals. It's a habit I purposely forced on myself a long time ago."

"Whatever for, lad?"

Circling his gaze, but playing it mostly on Anton Gavor, Apple said, "Well, the English are odd about animals. They don't like the treatment they think they get in circus acts. Myself, I believe that any way you can control an animal is fine. Any way at all."

The pause was over. Everyone began to talk at the same time. The topic, Apple realized, was a perennial. Even the Chinese juggler, who until now had spoken seldom, got up and joined in. Anton Gavor wore a smile. Apple was satisfied with what he had accomplished.

He was getting a second drink some minutes later when Tina appeared at his side. "I am going now," she said. "How tall you are."

"Leaving so early?"

"I have just found out we are thirteen. It is one of my superstitions."

"No, there're twelve of us," Apple said, looking around. "I counted earlier."

"And forgot to count yourself. People always do. Or, perhaps in this case, you forgot to include the servant." She moved past. "Good-bye, Apple."

"Good night, Tina."

"Do not forget that you promised to come and see me. In a day or two."

How much of that was whisky, and how much due to the message he had just conveyed?—Apple mused, watching Tina take leave of the host. But she did seem to approve of his tallness.

The party continued. It was some minutes before Apple realized that Anton Gavor was still present, that he had not left with Tina. Curious for more than one reason about the relationship, Apple supposed it was possible for it to be strictly business, at least from Tina's point of view.

He moved over to where the Hungarian and one of the trapeze artists were in a deep conversation. He stopped, and the talk dimmed, as someone said an urgent, "Listen. What's that?"

For two seconds there was nothing but silence. Then, from somewhere outside came a shout. It said, "Fire!"

Apple would not have thought it possible if he hadn't been a witness. The polite, languid guests erupted into shouting activity. No hundred-yard athlete ever responded faster to the gun than they did to the shout. Fat Sir Jasper sped to the door like a stripling bank robber. The others followed. Last out was the manservant, clutching a siphon of soda-water.

Apple stood alone. Walk, don't run, to the nearest exit, he had been telling himself. But now, the guests' shouts fading, he realized that the fire wasn't here. The people hadn't been thinking of themselves in their antic dash. It was aid they had in mind, not escape. *Fire* was the worst four-letter word you could use in a tenting world.

Apple put down his glass and hurried out, stumbling down the steps into darkness.

The big top seemed not to be in danger. At least, there was no glow to be seen from the huge hump that towered over everything. But canvas wasn't the only chink in the armour, Apple understood as he made his way through the maze. From ahead, above the clamour of voices, could be heard the revving of engines.

Living and storage trailers, trucks and cars and equipment—everything was parked closely together. This in part was for convenience; but mostly, Apple suspected, to satisfy a tribal instinct for survival against the outsider: townsman or thief or magistrate. Whatever, the proximity meant that if one unit went up in flames, they could all go.

Apple stumbled on. He was not alone. Other people constantly passed him, some old enough to be his grandparents. They were used to the twisting paths. He felt like a horse on a highway. Everyone who overtook him asked, "Whose is it?" He said, "Dunno."

Before him a space opened up. In the glare of headlights, people bustled. With engines roaring, vehicles were being edged away or reversed to trailers. A woman shepherded along a group of children in pajamas. Men were kicking away chocks and supports. Arvo the Finn, his jacket gone, was single-handedly pulling a large generator.

Briefly, Apple experienced a pang of regret at not being, in truth, a part of the community. He shook himself and went on, into one side of the space. From back there was coming the crackle of burning.

Apple joined in with a line of people. They moved quickly. Each person carried a water-receptacle of some kind, from large water-jack to kettle.

Apple came in bright view of the victim. It was a living trailer. The back end was busily on fire. The flames, rising high and sending out sparks, seemed impervious to the fire extinguishers that were being played on them by half-a-dozen men. Most of the fetched water was being tossed over surrounding vehicles, especially the matching trailer next door.

Which was when Apple recognised the victim. It was the unit shared by the male Hungarians, Anton Gavor and Tibor Polk.

Nick Stick stood on a box beside Tina's trailer. He was tall enough to empty onto its roof the containers being handed to him. But some of them he was unable to lift or lost half the water in the lifting.

Apple went over. Drawing the clown down, he took his place on the box, his role as soaker. The contents of receptacles large and small he sent swooshing over the roof. It was another of those infrequent moments in his life when he was proud and glad of his height.

Soon, the extinguishers began to get the best of their fight. The flames lowered. Sparks were reduced in number to isolated beams that rose high in the smoke. The vocal clamour changed in character; it took on a tone of victory. Water bearers came at a slower pace. The nearby revving of engines died away. Somebody laughed.

Half an hour later, Apple was in the backstage tent. So was everybody else, including children and babes in arms. There was a racket of cheery talk. Tea and ploughman sandwiches were being served. Again, Apple had felt that pang.

Amelia Earhart, still in business leathers and goggles, dripped water, as did dozens of others. The Chinese jugglers had been turned vaguely Negroid by smoke. Sir Jasper, beaming, was going around with a tray of tea mugs. The French acrobats were helping to cut sandwiches. His sad face wearing an attempt at a smile, Tibor Polk toured in offering everyone a handshake and abundant thanks.

Because his dark suit didn't show its sodden condition, Apple had helped the picture by taking off his tie and scuffling his hair. Also, covertly, he had put streaks of soot on his face. He told himself it was in the name of the mission.

Nick Stick came up with a tray. "Have a sandwich."

"Thanks. That was hunger-making work."

"Dirty work, you mean."

Apple raised his eyebrows. "Oh?"

"Leastways, that's what some people're saying."

Apple chewed and swallowed. "The fire was started deliberately?"

"You've got it," the clown said. "There were fine ashes under the trailer, as if a bloody great pile of paper and suchlike had been stuffed there."

"That wouldn't be a very sensible thing for anyone to do."

"Some people don't think of others. They think of money. Insurance, for instance."

"That idea probably comes from the Hungarians not being liked," Apple said. Intrigued by the thoughts of arson, he wanted to play it down. "But I notice that everyone pitched in to give a hand, regardless of that."

"It's the way we are," Nick Stick said. "But don't think this talk comes only from dislike. It was real funny for the fire to take hold like that, not to mention its peculiar resistance to the extinguishers."

Chemicals, Apple thought. The material for making drugs. He said, "Fire is a peculiar thing."

The clown gave his sideways nod. "Maybe it is. And maybe it isn't." He moved away. "See you."

His place was taken by Sir Jasper and the Finnish strong-man. The latter, as Apple helped himself to tea, began to talk about fires he had known on the big top circuit.

"Paris in the September of sixty-three," he said. "You will recall that one, Mr. Porter."

"No, I was already at school in England by then. In fact, I've never even heard of it. Was it a big one?"

"Well, no, not too very."

"The worst circus fire of all time," Apple said, "was in Hartford, Connecticut. A hundred and eighty-six people died. That was in the July of forty-four."

Sir Jasper Ranklin bobbed his head. "You're exactly right, lad. Exactly." It was obvious that he had forgotten having given Apple the information at breakfast time. He went on to talk of other tent show disasters.

In a minute, Apple excused himself. He had seen Anton Gavor moving through the dense crowd. As he neared, he himself was seen by the Hungarian, who made for him directly. His shaven head was dirty, his eyes were red, his suit was a mess.

He took Apple's hand in a short, hard shake. "I was looking for you. Tina wishes me to convey to you her thanks for your generous assistance."

Apple waved that aside. "Is she here?"

"No. She has retired for the night. Which is what I am about to do. Mr. Polk and I have found temporary shelter in a truck. Tomorrow we will assess the extent of the damage."

"You should have half a trailer left, anyway."

Anton Gavor lit a cigarette. Looking at Apple closely through the updrifting smoke he said, "I have heard of a rumour. People are whispering that the fire was caused intentionally. I don't agree. Do you, Mr. Porter?"

With surprise, Apple realized he was a suspect. That, or Anton was trying this on with everyone, hoping to shift attention from himself.

Carefully, Apple asked, "Is there any evidence to indicate arson?"

"None whatever. I think, myself, that it was an accident."

"Accidents will happen. One happened to me today. Some people might have seen it as being caused deliberately." He told of his experience with the dive-bomber, ending, "I don't think it could have been planned, do you?"

Anton shrugged one shoulder. "Was there any evidence to indicate interference?"

"No, none whatever."

There was a short silence. Looking at him closely again through smoke, Anton Gavor said, "Good night, Mr. Porter."

"Good night."

It was raining next morning. The water fell from grey, grim skies in the implacable way that is a celebrated feature of British summers. Tourists never believe it beforehand. Apple, as English as Cheddar cheese, could hardly believe it himself.

He sat in Wintertree's lobby and stared at the streaming windows. He had nothing else to do. It would be pointless for him to go to the showground. He would be soaked within seconds. No amount of nostalgia could explain his tramping about in the wet and mud. All he could do was wait for the sky to clear.

An hour went slowly by. Apple sat in frustration. He thought of arson, the questioning Finn, Anton, Tina saying, "Don't forget you promised to come and see me." When the proprietress brought him his suit, dried and pressed, Apple took it up to his room while musing that he could always buy a coat and an umbrella. But he didn't want to go through that expense account business again.

Down in the lobby, Apple sat through another hour of watching the rain. It seemed to be heavier, if anything. He realized that if he were really determined to go to the circus field, the weather wouldn't hold him back, which must mean there was something else on his mind. Some other task he ought to do.

The answer came to him with the appearance in the lobby of gap-tooth Jimmy. As the youth came toward him, letting show his love of all things glittery, Apple remembered Mavis Regland.

He got up quickly and went to the door.

In his dash to the station wagon, he got a fair drenching. His leather jacket, however, caught most of the rain. He took it off, dried his hair on the lining, and turned the heater up to high as he drove away. The windcheater he lay on the floor, by the heater's yawning mouth.

It was a slow drive for three-quarters of the way. Traffic crawled. Apple sat leaning forward over the steering wheel in order to see with decent clarity through the watery windshield: The wipers only had the one, turgid speed. Apple supposed that the Service gadget-boffins considered every contingency except the weather. Even the de-mister worked badly.

In Bath, the weather was as beautiful as were the old parts of the city. Apple drove around for a while before following signs to Chepton Vale, seven miles away. It was an overlarge village, with forty-odd shops siding its long main street. All the businesses were closed. It was noon.

Apple parked in the quietness and semi-desertion. His windcheater dry, he put it on as he walked to the nearest pub. Inside, it had a slim scattering of customers. The murmur of talk hushed until Apple had settled quietly on a stool at the bar, thus showing that he was not about to do anything to affront or entertain.

The barmaid was pretty, with dimples near her eyes as well as on the lower cheeks. Apple, after ordering a sherry on the rocks, said, "Do you serve food? Something smells good."

There was cottage pie or steak and kidney pudding. Apple ordered the pie. When it came, he paid and added a generous tip. The barmaid blushed. Somehow, on her, it looked fine.

Apple left the matter until he had finished eating. He lit a cigarette and drew the barmaid to him by tilting back his head. He asked, "Do you happen to know the Reglands?"

"I'll say," the girl said, laughing. "There's thousands of 'em in these parts. I was one myself before I got married. Which one would you be looking for?"

"A young one. Mavis."

"She's my cousin," the barmaid said with affection. "A real character, she is. You never know what she'll get up to next. Used to buzz around on a motorbike before she lost her licence.

68

Once she climbed up on the roof here and hung her panties on the TV mast."

"Yes, that sounds like the girl. A mutual friend asked me to call on her. Say hi."

"And not long back, believe it or not, she ran off with a circus."

"Really?" Apple said, laughing. "This one I have to meet. Could you give me her address, please?"

"Gladly," the barmaid said. "But I don't know if you can see her just now. She's sick."

Pacing the street, Apple waited for the stores to open. He bought a box of chocolates. Laughingly, nervous, he told the salesman, who hadn't asked, that his gift was for someone who had one of those trifling summer colds. It was nothing. Nothing at all.

Apple drove badly as he headed along second-class roads and lanes of no class whatever. Twice he got lost, once he arrived back in Chepton Vale. He was wondering if he should call in, contact Watkin, ask about the health of the operative who had volunteered to take Soma-2.

He imagined his superior saying urgently, "Thank God you called. There's no time to lose. We can save you if you get back here quickly." It made Apple feel better. The idea of Angus Watkin displaying urgency was absurd.

The farm lay at the end of a rutted lane. Cows came ambling across the yard as Apple got out of his car. They had the same untidy but friendly look as the farmhouse, the door of which was standing open to the sun.

Apple leaned inside and called, "Hello!" At the far end of a flagstone passage, a woman appeared. Middle-aged, pudgy, she wiped her hands on a sacking apron while strolling forward.

69

She said, "We've got no eggs today, young man."

"I came to see Mavis," Apple said. "A friend of hers asked me to bring her these chocolates."

"Well now, isn't that nice. Thank you. I'll see that she gets them."

"And I have to say hello to her for this friend. I have to give her a message."

"She's ill," the woman said. "Took to her bed yesterday morning. Sudden, it was. It's not like her at all. She never ails."

"Has she had a doctor?"

"Wouldn't. You have no idea how strong-willed that girl is."

"Listen," Apple said. "I really would like to see her, if you'd let me."

"Me, I've got nothing to do with it," the woman said, as if proudly. Turning her head, she directed a shout up the stairs: "Mavis! There's a young fella here to visit you!"

After a pause, a voice answered, "Who is it?"

The woman looked at Apple. "Who are you?"

"Jimmy."

"His name's Jimmy! He's got a box of chocolates! They look like hard centres!"

"I know lots of Jimmies," the girl said. "Which one is it?"

Apple told her mother, "I'm from the circus."

The woman shouted up the stairs, "This young man's from that circus of yours!"

From above, silence. When the girl spoke again, her voice had lost tone. She said, "I'm sick. I've got to get some sleep now."

Apple stepped inside and brushed by the woman, telling her quietly, "I'll just slip up and give her the present. Also the message. Won't stay more than a couple of ticks. You go on with your work."

"I'll show you the way."

"I'll find it myself. And this message, it's private."

The woman sniffed. "Oh well. Private. That lets *me* out." She jerked her head. "It's the first door you come to."

Apple took the stairs in five strides. The door was ajar. He pushed it open and entered a small bedroom, arriving at the foot of a brass bedstead. Propped in it on pillows, surrounded by magazines, was Mavis, an average-pretty girl with frizzy yellow hair. Her earrings were miniature razor blades. She wore no cosmetics apart from heavy black lines around her eyes, which made her look terrified.

Drawing the covers chin high, she asked a faint, "What d'you want?"

"To say hello," Apple said, smiling. He held the box like an auctioneer's assistant showing a Renoir. "Chocs."

"Thank you."

He put the box among the magazines. "How do you feel?"

"Awful. I feel real bad. I want to go to sleep."

Apple told himself that she looked fine, apart from the eyes. He asked about pain, nausea, other symptoms. Mavis, rolling negatives with her head, kept repeating, "I just feel bad, that's all."

Apple grasped the brass rail. He wondered: Now what?

The girl asked, "Who did you say sent you?"

"An anonymous admirer. He's had a thing about you ever since that party at Dorchester."

"Christ," the girl said plaintively. "He must be mad. I made a right fool of myself."

"It wasn't your fault."

She rolled her head again. "It wasn't. That's the God's truth. It was that rotten Anton. *He* did it. First off he gave me something strong to drink. Rum, I think it was. Then he hypnotised me. I don't remember a thing after that."

She twitched, stared, licked her lips. "Anton's very nice, actually. I like him."

"I heard that you told some startling home truths."

"I heard the same. But I couldn't help myself. I didn't mean any harm. And I was only saying what I really believed. I mean, I wasn't making anything up, just to be rotten. I've got nothing against Sir Jasper. He treated me decent."

"But he fired you," Apple said.

"Can't blame him for that, not after what I said about him."

"I was told what it was, but I can't recall it at the moment."

"I said I thought he was a pansy," the girl said, shuddering. "As gay as the flowers of May, I said. I said he was always watching those Chinese boys, and I told about the time I'd seen him peeping through their trailer window."

Apple nodded slowly and thoughtfully. He could hear Watkin saying, "Forget it, Porter." But he couldn't, if only because Sir Jasper Ranklin was the unlikeliest operative for British Intelligence that he could imagine. If the signs were right.

"I think I'll go to sleep now," Mavis said. She still had the covers to her chin. She still looked terrified.

Apple was intrigued. He found that he had a notion trying to form at the back of his mind, made up of several bits and pieces. While allowing the try to continue, he followed the Training Four adage, *When you have nothing to say, look confident.*

Mavis's return look was the reverse of that. It deteriorated as the seconds ticked by. Abruptly she blurted, "You're a cop, aren't you?"

Apple sighed. Now the notion was fully formed. He said gently, "You left a clue."

Mavis had raised the covers so that only her eyes were showing. The fear had been real all along. Faintly she asked, "What was it?"

"I'm not at liberty to divulge that."

The girl whimpered. Apple asked, "Whose motorbike did you use?"

"A boyfriend's."

"Does he know about you preparing an alibi of being sick?"

"Yes, but I didn't tell him what I was going to do. I wasn't even sure myself till I got there. The idea just came to me."

"People could have died," Apple said, still gentle.

The girl's hands tightened on the sheet. "I didn't think about that until afterwards. Honest to Christ, I didn't."

"You only wanted to hurt Anton Gavor."

"Yes."

"You didn't. His insurance will take care of the fire damage. He might even get a new trailer out of this. You've probably done him a favour. But think of what might have happened. Think about being charged with manslaughter. Think about children being trapped in burning trailers."

Apple went on in this vein. He wasn't playing a part. He felt appalled by the girl's act, even though it had been based on stupidity, thoughtlessness. His emotions urged him to ease up, have compassion on the culprit, who had started to shiver, but he fought gamely back.

Mavis interrupted by sitting up. "I'm going to be sick."

"You needn't put on a performance for me," Apple said. "I'm not a policeman."

"Don't care. I feel ill."

"You didn't leave any clues, so far as I know. You're safe."

"I'm ill," Mavis gasped. "Honest. I need a doctor."

It was late when Apple started back to Taunton. The Regland farm having no telephone, and no vehicle available, he himself had driven into the village. He was glad to help: His sympathy had come on strongly, he felt guilt, he wanted to know verdict and prognosis.

He had followed the doctor's car back to the farm. During the examination he waited downstairs. The doctor, who looked like a yokel in Harvest Thanksgiving tweeds, came down to say that it appeared as if young Mavis had influenza. "A week in bed and she'll be as good as new."

Apple had probed. He learned nothing more and left it when the doctor started to look at him suspiciously. Going out to the station wagon, he decided that Mavis could be suffering from remorse and fear, compounded by a cold reaction to the fast motorcycle drive she had taken when her mother thought she was in bed.

It was dark by the time Apple drove into the parking field, having stopped in Wells to eat. Cars were lined up in long ranks. The evening performance of the circus had been on for more than an hour. The fairground stalls were bright and busy.

Although the rain had ended long since, underfoot was soggy. Apple circled pools of water as he went along the right-hand side of the avenue of attractions. Their operators waved or called out greetings to him as he passed. His help last night had given him the final push into acceptance, he realized with professional and private pleasure.

Going into the behind scenes, Apple headed for the Hungarian units. He went carefully in the darkness. When he turned around what he thought was the last truck, he saw he had been mistaken. He circled the next—and was mistaken again.

But then he realized what was wrong. The maze to which he had almost become accustomed had been re-formed. All the vehicles in this section that had been moved clear of the fire last night had been brought back, but into different positions.

It took Apple another five minutes of fumbling before he

came to the twin grey trailers. Both were in darkness. The nearest had a surrealistic appearance. Its end seemed to have melted.

Apple stood and waited. He was about to light a cigarette, but thoughts of fire made him change his mind. It was after he had put the packet back in his pocket that he heard the hiss.

He looked around. He could see nothing in the dimness. The sound came again. It was now recognisable as being of human origin. It was someone saying, "Psst."

Apple went in that direction, his nerves growing taut. After another hiss, the voice changed to words. It whispered hoarsely, "This way."

Apple went on. He could still see no one among the vehicles. He came to a truck, a ramp leading up to the open half of its double door at the back. The interior was dark.

"In here," the voice said.

Apple remembered that the Hungarians had fixed themselves up with other accommodations. He stepped onto the ramp. In a low voice he asked, "Who is it?"

The voice, unidentifiable even as to sex because of the whisper, said, "This way. Come on."

Apple went up the ramp with care. He reached the doorway, touched it with his hands at either side. The interior was still as black as old tar. Again the voice came, urging him to enter.

He did so.

Apple yelled as the door hit him in the back. He pitched forward onto his hands and knees. The door closed. He could see no better than if he had his eyes tightly shut.

"What the hell is this?" he snapped.

There was no answer.

His nerves jangled, Apple got up by the wall. Touching it, he felt his way back to the door. Blindly he skimmed both hands

75

over the spread of metal; all over, not simply near the faint split down the middle. There was no handle.

He paused. He could hear breathing. Swiftly he swung around to put his shoulders to the metal. "Who's here?" he asked loudly. "What's going on?"

Still no answer. The breathing went on. It was coming from more than one pair of lungs. There was also a vocal murmur.

His eyes adjusting, Apple saw patches of light. They were coming, he saw after another few seconds, from square holes in the upper part of the truck walls. The interior grew a shade less dark. And Apple, stiffening, was able to make out the top silhouettes of two figures.

"Who's that?" he said.

The figures were standing about six feet away. They had an attitude of menace. That was due to the darkness, Apple assured himself. He said, "Anton? Tibor? Is that you?"

Still no answer, except the breathing.

Apple remembered his cigarette lighter. He fumbled it out of his pocket, flicked it on. He gagged in fear. The lighter dropped from his hand and went out as it hit the floor.

During the brief illumination, Apple had seen the two figures clearly. They were gorillas.

Gasping, Apple pressed himself against the metal. In his mind he gabbled a self-warning not to alarm the animals. He must not cry out. He must not shout for help. He must not pound on the door.

Now Apple noticed the smell. He hadn't before because that sense was being ignored in favour of sight, touch, and hearing. The smell was rancid.

With a shuffling sway, the gorillas came a fraction closer. Apple clenched his knees to stop their trembling. Faintly he

76

could see the animals' faces; the sunken eyes, cavernous noses, huge mouths.

The square holes above, Apple thought. Could he get through? He glanced up, hardly daring to take his eyes off the gorillas. But the glance was enough to show him that there was no escape that way. The holes were just about large enough for a man to get his head through, and, Apple thought bitterly, whisper an invitation to come in.

Again the two animals edged a little closer. With them came the stink. Their breathing was louder.

Hope surged in Apple as he remembered Soma-2. It surely must be used on the animals for the ring performance. That wasn't long over. The drug would still be having its effect.

Apple crashed his fists backwards against the door, at the same time shouting, "Help!"

He shuddered. The word died at the back of his throat.

With the sudden racket, the gorillas had jerked as if pushed. Now they growled. They swung their long arms. They lifted their heads. They showed large, sharp fangs.

These creatures weren't drugged, Apple felt sickeningly sure. Their response had been too sharp, he thought. In the ring, their every movement had been languid and easy. Soma-2, if used, had worn off. Or maybe this pair hadn't even been in the act tonight. They could be stand-bys.

Giving low grunts, the gorillas swayed themselves closer. Their fur seemed to be bristling. Now they were less than five feet away. They could almost touch him if they stretched, Apple knew.

He let his knees have their tremble. He needed to think. And fast. The animals could attack at any second, for with every second that went by they were growing more sure of themselves, more active. When he had first come in, they had been motionless. This could only be a bad sign.

Apple was already beginning to bend before the idea of the cigarette lighter took firm hold in his mind.

Flame. That was the one element feared by all creatures, from mice to elephants and on into the human variety. If he could get the lighter.

Apple shot down multiple glances as he continued to lower himself slowly, slowly into a squat. His lighter was silver. Even so, he was unable to pick it out in the lower darkness. He stopped looking down. He had to keep his eyes on the gorillas.

They became as tall as he was as he went on with the achingly slow movement downward; then taller; then taller still when, in addition to his sinking, they came another shuffle closer.

Apple froze his stance. He wondered if it was only his unusual height that had made them so docile when he had entered the truck. They were used to men of about their own size. Now they saw something that was more familiar. They even had a height advantage.

But he had to have flame, Apple told himself. And if they attacked, he would then be free to scream for help, which was sure to come immediately, at once, straightaway, instantly, right now.

No matter how much Apple insisted, he didn't believe it. But it did help him bear the feeling of being totally defenceless as he started squatting again. He went on down. The grunting, swaying gorillas seemed to grow immense.

Mouth open and dry, stark gaze up, Apple came within reach of the floor. He held his pose there. Balance kept by the door at his back, he began to fluster his fingers across the floor. They met nothing.

The animals came closer. They were grunting continually

now. Their breathing was short and raspy. They towered over Apple as they swayed and looked ready to fall on top of him at any moment.

His left hand found the lighter. He picked it up, fumbled, lost hold. His fingers were drooling sweat. He searched with his right, scored, picked up the lighter. Holding it with both hands, he thumbed down the lever. The flame sprang to life.

Both gorillas hissed. Apple heard this in panic. He thought the attack was on. With the sudden glare on his eyes, he could see nothing. Then, two seconds later, his vision recovered from the shock, he saw that the animals had moved a pace backwards.

The relief of that for Apple was countered by him also being able to see the great shaggy creatures in all their petrifying size, brute force, and ugliness.

His thumb, slick with sweat, slipped off the lever. The light went out. Again he heard a hiss. It was followed by a growling and the noise of movement. These went on as he jabbed his thumb repeatedly over the lighter's lever.

The spark connected, the wick took alight. This time Apple's eyes did better. There was only a short break before he was able to see. The gorillas were holding. He extended the lighter toward them. They moved a pace back.

Panting, Apple continued to hold out his arm. His panic began to slow down, but only as a frightened man, running, relaxes from the ultimate effort. Pulses were beating rapidly at each side of his neck. His painfully taut attention was divided between the hovering animals and his slippery thumb on the lever.

The door opened.

Apple found himself falling backwards. He flung out his arms for balance, failed to hold it, went right over—and out of the truck.

Into his vision, for the second time at the circus, came a view that was upside down. This, however, was not a boy's face. It was a man, walking away quickly, but not quickly enough to prevent Apple recognising him by the mane of white hair.

Apple rolled down the ramp and onto the wet grass.

Wet or dry, green or purple, Apple didn't care. He lay flat, face down, and hugged himself to the outdoors. After a few seconds he even got a mouthful of grass and began to chew it. He rolled over luxuriously.

The cigarette lighter was still in his hand. He wasn't surprised. Nothing short of a bullet, he thought, would have made him loose his grip. About to put the lighter away, Apple remembered the door.

He leapt up. He went back to the foot of the ramp. As before, he could see nothing inside the truck. Going cautiously partway up, he leaned forward with outstretched arm and flicked on the lighter.

He could see the gorillas, which were in the same place and stance as before. He could also see, after looking them up and down, that, as an extra precaution against escape, each was held inside the truck by a strap around its left ankle. The gorillas couldn't get out, but they could reach the door. They could have reached him.

Apple went down off the ramp. Fire or no fire, he felt he had to have a smoke. He lit up and took deep, hungry drags. If he ever did give up cigarettes, he thought, which he ought to one of these days, maybe next week, he would certainly never give up lighters.

Apple was calm by the time he killed the stub, with care. He went on, took two wrong turnings among the rearranged vehicles, and then came to the backs of the twin trailers. In Tina's, lights glowed softly from behind heavy curtains.

Apple mused that while the identity of the one who had lured him into the gorilla trap was in doubt, he was sure of who had saved him. Although, of course, it could have been the same person. Whichever, there was more to Tibor Polk than met the eye.

Softly, Apple went close to the occupied trailer. Voices were coming from inside. He could hear them only as a drone. They stayed that way even when he pressed his ear right on the glass of the window. But he was able to distinguish that the drones belonged to three separate people. He went to the next window along.

Voices rose. But they were coming from out here, not inside. Apple got himself away from the trailer just in time, before the couple came in sight. They were arguing about which had more protein value, a steak or a bottle of stout. They exchanged greetings with Apple as he passed them on his acted journey along the same lane.

Couple gone, he doubled back. He noted now that the strongest light from Tina's showed at the end, where it closely met the matching end of the burned trailer. They almost touched. Blocking off both rear windows from view, so that the light was seen only as a glow above, were various items of equipment. They obviously had been put there after being rescued from the fire. Even if there wasn't the same barrier at the other side, Apple didn't want to risk being there, where the door was.

Delicately, he began lifting down a box. He stopped as a whistling sounded, darted off around the corner of a nearby truck, and stayed out of sight until the youth had taken his whistle by. Apple was glad he had never liked that particular tune.

He returned to the trailers. This time he hadn't got started on removing objects when the couple's voices began growing again.

He went back to the truck. The couple went by. The man had lost the argument. They were going to have steak.

This was going to be no good, Apple thought as he came out of hiding. He needed to be where he wouldn't be interrupted. Which meant under the trailer, or on the roof, or . . .

Smiling, he went to the damaged unit. He stepped quietly through blackened wreckage and over to where the jagged-edged floor began. It creaked as he stepped up onto it. Before him was an interior door, swinging open. He went through and along a short passage. It led into a room with bunk beds, though everything had been removed except the frames. The window was bare.

He stepped across to it softly. Now he was looking directly through into Tina's trailer. Mere feet away, at a table, sat Tina and Anton Gavor and Tibor. They were drinking soup.

Suddenly realizing that they could see him with equal clarity, if they glanced this way, Apple shot down to one knee. He had noticed one point that excited him: Tina's rear window was slightly open.

The window beside him had two screw-catches. They were at the bottom of the frame. Apple twisted one loose, then the other. Hoping the movement wouldn't be seen, he gradually eased the window open, creating a two-inch gap. He listened there.

The chinking of spoons was louder than the voices, which came at intervals, and sounded like mere comments of appreciation on the food. Speech still made only a drone.

Apple tried to get his ear closer to the gap—though without letting his head show around the window's edge. In twisting, he overbalanced. He landed heavily in a sit, making a tremendous crash of noise.

Frozen, mouth open, Apple glared at the window above him.

He daren't move, but knew that he would be seen if one of the trio stood up and looked through the two windows.

The clink of cutlery on bowls, after a pause, went on. Anton spoke. His voice came clearly. He said, "If bits of that ceiling keep falling, you're going to be awake all night."

Tina answered. What she said was the same drone as before. That was unimportant to Apple. He was hardly listening in any case and had forgotten the relief of having had the noise explained away.

The hairs were prickling on the nape of his neck: Anton Gavor had spoken in Russian.

Carefully, his mind a hive of busyness, Apple inched himself back into position by the window. By listening acutely, he established that Russian was being used by all three, although individual words remained vague. Tina and Anton spoke the language perfectly. Tibor had an accent.

Five minutes passed. The soup was finished. Among sounds of movement, Apple distinguished the words *cheese* and *knife* and *appetite*. The trio munched and mumbled. More time passed.

In spates, the voices became clearer. Anton talked about the fire. He didn't like it. He was worried. To Tibor Polk he said something harsh about the gorillas. Apple heard his own name, heard Tibor use *comrade*, and heard Tina say, her voice on a clear note with, it seemed, exasperation, "But I don't think he *is* British Intelligence."

CHAPTER 3

Apple didn't try to stop his blushing. No image of sauna bath or fur coat did he conjure up. He let the heat bloom, the prickling rampage. The blush was well and truly deserved. He should suffer it.

Creeping quietly out of the burnt trailer, shock gone, shame in, Apple sneered at himself that he ought to have seen the overall picture long ago. It was obvious. He had been slow and naïve. He had been a bumbling amateur.

Which, of course, was why he was here. He had been sent out into the espionage field on a Fools-rush.

Where angels fear to tread, that was where your inexperienced agent was inclined to go rushing, Apple knew. The greenhorn would cheerfully try tricks the pro would scorn as old-fashioned, but which, gratuitously, the other side would view as too corny to be the work of an agent, and therefore accept as genuine.

For instance, if a man dressed as a mechanic walked into an embassy's garage saying the ambassador had called him in to look at his car, chances are he would be allowed to go ahead, without anyone bothering to check with higher-ups. No foreign operative would be insane enough to think that anyone would fall for that old gag. Only a faceless one on a Fools-rush would be innocent enough to try it.

Apple walked through the behind-scenes maze. He went

slowly. His blushes lessened to pink, revived to red. They were on their way out as he left the vehicles behind and headed for the gate. Night's activities over, the fair was dark and silent.

Apple got in the station wagon. He relaxed and lit a cigarette. The whole set-up grew clearer in his mind as he smoked.

Appleton Porter, he mused, had been sent in for two reasons. One, his Fools-rush tactics, which could pay off where others might fail. Two, his ignorance as to what was going on, for the pro might give it away by being too clever, or have it drawn out of him by means of torture or the drug.

Apple could understand the reasoning of Angus Watkin, but that didn't stop him from thinking evilly of the man.

Apple started the motor. He drove out of the empty field and turned toward town. Shame gone, he was beginning to feel excited. He was, after all, on a true mission. Tina Koves, Tibor Polk, and Anton Gavor were Communist agents, and they were playing a very neat game.

Apple admired the thinking, the planning. An act with a travelling circus was beautifully far removed from the usual lanes of espionage work. The act drew a lot of attention. Posing as Free Hungarians was fine so long as they avoided using Magyar, which Tina and Anton spoke imperfectly. By claiming to be of non-circus stock, the trio would not have needed to research the tenting world, would not need to explain why they had no acquaintances in it. This same claim would allow them to act the snob, keep from getting too friendly with their colleagues.

They knew, of course, about the Chinese-watcher. He, they made sure, got hold of the pop bottle during or after the game of truth. They knew that it and the game's outcome would arrive on the right desk. All they had to do then was sit back and wait for British Intelligence to send someone in disguised as something else. The trio, two Hammers and a Sickle, would rise in the KGB for the smooth way they had managed.

Apple thought of the dive-bomber ride, the GO AWAY note, and this evening's visit to the gorillas. The trio wanted rid of him as a mere nuisance even if he wasn't an enemy agent. His continued presence would assure them that he was prepared to take risks.

It was all perfectly clear to Apple except on one glaring point. Why were the KGB trying to give British Intelligence this marvellous truth drug?

It was a fine morning. Apple felt the same, fine and fresh. He left the hotel before breakfast and bought himself a jar of lemon marmalade. He had it on his toast. This, his favourite snack, helped him with his thinking, as always. He got everything in neat order, and decided that the worst was over. The rest was going to be enjoyably easy. His biggest problem would be in not letting the trio see or sense that he was onto their game.

Apple told himself that if he had any brain, he would bow out of the scene. He would pretend he had had enough after his experience with the gorillas, and let Angus Watkin send in another faceless one, who couldn't give away knowledge that he didn't have. Apple decided not to be brainy.

Not forgetting his marmalade, he left the dining room to the lying salesmen and went upstairs. In his room he picked up the telephone and got an outside line. He asked directory enquiries for the number of the doctor in Chepton Vale. Making contact, he asked:

"Anything new on Mavis Regland, doctor?"

"I haven't been on my rounds yet. It's only nine-thirty. Give me a call later."

Disconnecting, Apple wondered about the pair of gorillas last night. Were they needed because the troupe had to be constantly replaced due to illness or death? He didn't take it any further.

Out of the hotel, to prove to himself how well he felt, Apple went for a long, vigorous walk. The rising sun warm, he took off his leather jacket and slung it over his shoulder. He whistled, which he broke off on recognising the tune as the one he had heard last night.

Apple questioned if he was being tailed; if he could have been so ever since first making himself known at the circus. Going down an alley, he waited out of sight. No one came in cautious pursuit.

Apple went back to the car, got in, and headed out of town. More confident now of acceptance, he ignored the empty field and turned into the other. He steered around to the back. Parking, he went into the cluster of vehicles. At the twin trailers, he circled to the front.

In a canvas chair, under the awning, sat Tina. She wore a white towelling robe. Her braids were coiled up on top of her head like an Austrian loaf. Seeing Apple she smiled and said, her voice louder than necessary, it seemed:

"Oh, it is you, Apple. The valiant hero of the fire. Have you come to visit me?"

"Good morning. Yes." He went under the awning, which was pitted with burn holes. "What a beautiful day."

They talked weather, agreeing that in Britain it was as eccentric as the British. "It may have caused them to be that way in the first place," Apple said. He needed to remind himself that this delicious creature was a hard-gutted Sickle. He wished, for the mission's sake, that he could forget it.

"As a matter of fact," Tina said, "I was on the point of tanning my body. Sun bathing, you call it? How apt. Perhaps you would like to help me with the cream—yes?"

"Yes," Apple said, briefly forgetting.

"Come in, please."

He followed her inside, into a small living area. The drapes were drawn, making it pleasantly cool and dim. Apple noted a closet door and another one that, like in the matching trailer, led to a bedroom. He wondered, apropos of Tina's loud welcome, if Tibor or Anton, or both, were hiding behind those doors.

"Sit down, please, Apple."

He sat on the couch. There was silence as Tina took off her robe, tossed it aside and reached to a shelf for a tube of suntan cream. She wore a white bikini. At close range, her body was more startlingly sensational than when seen in the ring. Her navel was as lewd as a wanton's heavy-lidded eye.

Talking generalities, Tina began to put cream on her legs. She used both hands, languidly rubbing them up and down, bending low for the shins but concentrating mostly on the thighs. She circled, twisting this way and that. The voluptuousness of the act was wasted neither on Apple's mind nor his body.

He mused, trying to be cold, the pro, that Tina might herself be a faceless one. Where his own speciality was language, hers could be sex. There was no doubting her skill—at least, in projection.

Tina straightened. She asked, "Would you put cream on my back for me, please, Apple?"

"Of course," he said, getting up. "And I'll put your robe away for you in this clothes closet, if you like. Or in the bedroom."

"No no, I shall be needing it again shortly. Here." She gave him the tube of cream. "All my back, please." In turning around, she reached behind and unfastened the catch of her bikini top. The two strips of white strap dangled. Tina kept her elbows tight in, her hands high on her chest.

Apple put cream on both palms. He began to spread it lightly across the smooth shoulders. It came as no surprise to him to realize that even the back of Tina's neck looked erotic.

He wished the main door wasn't standing wide open. He wished he could stop forgetting that he was on a mission. He wished he could act like a pro.

Tina asked, "What are you thinking about, Apple?"

"Gorillas," he said. "Do you use the same five animals all the time?"

"Oh, yes. They are young and healthy. However, we do keep a pair in reserve, for emergencies."

"I see."

"I am pleased that you want to talk business."

"Business?"

Tina said, "Show business."

"Ah." Apple went on rubbing, going down past the shoulder blades. Her skin felt like silk. He murmured another, "Ah."

"Can you reach? I am too small. Perhaps I should stand on a box. But no, it will be the same thing if you kneel—yes?"

"I suppose."

"Kneel, Apple."

He got down to his knees. The shoulder blades were at eye level, and a foot away. He smoothed his hands down, thumbs nuzzling the spine, finger ends curling around the tiny waist. Think pro, he told himself as he rubbed lower, nearing the cleavage that showed above the tight white briefs. Think of Anton hiding in the bedroom. Think of a camera. Think mission.

"Thank you," Tina said. "Now the front. You will need more cream, I believe, Apple."

He turned away to get the tube. His hands were unsteady as he loaded them with lotion. He turned back—and twitched. Tina had removed her bikini top. Apart from the briefs, she was naked. Her pouting breasts jutted close to Apple's face. Tina sent them higher and firmer by casually lifting her arms to clasp the nape of her neck.

"It is obvious," she said, gazing lazily at the ceiling, "that you are genuine."

"Oh?" He lifted his hands and started to spread the cream on her upper chest.

"A genuine child of the circus, I mean. You are a Bohemian. Otherwise you would be shocked by my nudity."

Apple swallowed. He rubbed downward, lost his nerve at the last second, drew his hands around the sides of the breasts. He coated her stomach, telling himself:

Think Sickle. Think KGB. Think Angus Watkin.

With a shudder of indrawn breath, Apple moved his hands upward. They slid smoothly onto the jutting mounds, which he began to gently circle. They glistened with cream. He treated his palms to the rich brown nipples.

Trying hard, he said in a shaky voice, "I want to talk to Anton."

Tina said soothingly, "Of course you do, Apple." Her tone was a croon.

"I—I want to tell him that the fire . . ." He stopped himself. He could not, he realized, mention Mavis. That would be getting too close to the pop bottle. Why wasn't he thinking straight?

"What about the fire, Apple?"

Diligently, tenderly, he went on massaging the pliant breasts. He mumbled, "What?"

"The fire next door."

Apple managed, "I agree with Anton that it was an accident."
"Oh," Tina said. "Good."

Was it his imagination, or had her voice become lower, huskier? He tried to counter that wild hope with remembering the whispered invitation to enter the gorilla truck. It didn't work. Most of his brains were in his hands. He thumbed the taut nipples gently.

Tina said, "I think you also want to tell Anton the truth."
"About what?" he probably said.

"About you, Apple. About what you are. You are really an animal trainer—yes?"

He came back from the erotic far enough to realize that this was the approach the KGB would expect an agent to take. He would offer to buy the secret of the act. Apple left again. He didn't care.

He assumed it must have been his answer to the question, which he had no knowledge of giving, that made Tina now step away. Had he said the wrong thing? Letting his arms drop, he watched dreamily as Tina put on her robe.

She tied the belt with a flourish, whirled, and said, "Thank you for your help. Next, we will have a little drink."

Apple got shakily up. He was demoralised by his failure to play the pro. "No, thanks," he said, gasping. "Something to do. Back later. Excuse me." He moved to the door and blundered out.

Shattered, Apple sat in the car, on the passenger side. He sprawled with his head lying back on the seat, his legs folded against the dashboard. He felt incapable of rousing his body. Only with difficulty did he nudge his mind into functioning.

Tina, he thought drearily, had given him every opportunity to make his pitch, and he had ignored that in favour of acting like a smitten, sex-crazed schoolboy. He ought to call in at once and have himself pulled out of the assignment. He was a mess, a failure.

In absently wiping his cream-slick hands on his jeans, Apple recalled the feel of Tina's breasts. He smiled. That and his shift of thoughts made him furious. He sat up. He told himself that the Service was, after all, one hundred per cent right in not using him in the field. It was work for men, not boys.

Apple was staring gloomily ahead, five minutes later, when he remembered that he had refused a drink from Tina and had done so in some confusion. Which, of course, would make them fairly sure that he was a British agent, for otherwise why would he be wary of a drink?

A clever move, that, Apple thought.

A tap came on the car window. Apple looked around. Peering in at him was white-haired Tibor Polk. Apple slid across behind the steering wheel and rolled the window down. He said a pleasant:

"Hello, Tibor. It's a beautiful day."

"How do you do," the Hungarian said. His face was showing nervousness as well as the usual sorrow. He glanced behind him in both directions. "Can we talk?"

Apple reached for the door handle. "Certainly."

"No. Not here."

"Just as you like. Where?"

"Anywhere away from this place," Tibor Polk said. He looked around again. "Somewhere private."

Apple said, "We could go to my hotel room."

"That will do perfectly."

One minute later Apple was driving off with the Hungarian beside him, huddled small inside his green smock, his head turned so that he could see behind. Not until they were out on the road did he sit up straight.

He said, "Thank you."

"No, I must thank you. I wanted to speak to someone. Either you or Anton Gavor."

"Yes. It is time we put the cards on the table."

"We must be open with one another."

"Exactly, Mr. Porter."

Apple drove on. The reasoning, he mused, was that he would trust Tibor because he was the one who had done the rescue bit from the gorilla truck. Which might have been the motive for its use to begin with. All very devious and typical.

From the edge of his vision, Apple glanced at the older man's face. He thought he must be a brilliant actor. His features were full of a plaintive sadness. He looked as kind as Anton looked cold.

Nothing more was said until they were walking into the lobby, when Apple asked, "Shall I get something to drink to take up with us?"

"Well, a coffee for me, perhaps."

Apple went to the kitchen, where the proprietor obliged with two coffees. Apple carried the tray as he led the way upstairs and into his room. Tibor closed the door.

He said, "Yes, we can talk here."

"Sit down. Make yourself at home."

There was the bed or an upright chair. Between stood a small, round-topped table. Apple put the tray there as Tibor sat on the bed's edge. He asked for a cigarette. They both lit up.

Sitting on the chair and leaning forward, Apple said, "Okay, here's the table."

"I beg your pardon?"

"For putting our cards on, Tibor."

The Hungarian nodded. He looked toward the door. "Had that better be locked, do you think?"

"If it makes you feel happier," Apple said, "yes, of course." He got up, went to the door and slid across the paint-coated bolt. He turned as Tibor was aligning the tray neatly in the centre of the round table.

Apple returned to his seat and sat. He asked, "There isn't a chance that anyone would want to follow us, is there?"

"I do not know. Why do you ask?"

"Well, it seems to me that as I was coming back with the coffee, I saw someone standing across the street. He looked familiar, like a man I'd seen at the circus."

Tibor looked at the window. "Really?"

"Maybe I was mistaken."

"And possibly you were not." He got up and went across the room.

Instantly, Apple lifted the table and gave it one half revolution. He had it back on the floor again even before the older man had reached the window.

Apple picked up his coffee and sipped. "See anyone?"

After a moment Tibor said, "There is no one I recognise." He came back to the bed and sat down. "Well now."

"Let's get this coffee out of the way first."

"Yes, of course."

"I hate coffee when it's cold."

Tibor sipped. He pulled a face. He said, "It is my own fault. I ought to have told you that I did not take sugar."

"The sugar will give you energy," Apple said. Encouragingly, he drank.

Tibor looked embarrassed. "It was ill-mannered of me to mention the sugar." He lifted the cup and drained it.

Apple did the same with his own. "And now," he said, "I believe that we are going to have a real, good, heart-to-heart talk."

"Yes, we are, Mr. Porter. We most assuredly are."

Apple stubbed his cigarette in his saucer. "I think we'll be able to come to terms." It made him proud that he was acting so casually when he was about to get all the information he wanted from a Hammer, but especially an answer to the riddle of why the KGB were going to such great lengths to give Soma-2 to the British, for surely his coffee had been spiked with it when he had gone to lock the door.

Tibor Polk put his cigarette out. "I am sure, Mr. Porter," he said, "that we will meet no difficulties." His brow began to swell like a balloon. It bloomed out to the size of a football, then shrank again to normal, but went on shrinking. Soon he only had a plateau that was on a level with his eyebrows and ears. After holding there briefly, the rest of his head began to shrivel. It went from sight, the last hank of white hair sneaking down into his collar.

From that empty space, Tibor's voice said, "I think you had better lie on the floor, Mr. Porter."

Beautiful, Apple thought. What an utterly charming room, with those friendly little wrinkles in the wallpaper, those torn fringes on the lampshade, that crack in the door. And Tibor, his friend, the most wonderful person in the world. How great it was for them to be here together. And this rug. It was only the most comfortable in all creation, that's all, as soft and yielding as two mattresses.

"So they gave you the drug in your sherry, did they, Apple? That's fascinating. Please do go on."

Happily, Apple continued his story. He told of waking in the cell, of the short fight with Albert, of being taken to see Angus

Watkin and hearing the tape of what he had said while under the influence of that drug.

"We're calling it Soma-2, by the way," Apple said.

"Thank you."

"I thought you might find that rather interesting, Tibor, for the name comes from . . ."

"Yes, Apple," Tibor said gently. "But please go on with your fascinating tale of this mission." He moved a pocket-size tape recorder closer to the edge of the table.

Apple left nothing out, not even the way the station wagon had been given a spread of soil and a couple of seed boxes. He went on, describing everything he had seen, thought, and felt since coming to the circus.

He asked, "I'm not boring you, am I?"

"No, Apple. Not in the least. What happened after you got away from the gorillas?"

"After *you* let me get away, Tibor. Let's not forget that. I never shall. Ever."

"Thank you."

"Well, it was then," Apple said, "that the whole picture changed. I sneaked into the fire-damaged trailer and listened at the back window. I heard you and Tina and Anton talking. Russian. That was a surprise, let me tell you. With that, and other things that were said, I realized that you were all KGB. Was I right?"

"Anton and Tina are, yes. I am not."

"I knew somebody was."

"I can tell you, you see, because you will not remember any of this afterwards."

"Really?" Apple said. "Yes, I am forgetful at times. Would you like to hear how I faked the memory test during my training days?"

"I would love to, yes, but not at the moment. Let us get back to when you were listening to our conversation. The whole picture changed, you said."

"Yes. I realized that the entire circus thing was an elaborate set-up arranged by the KGB, who *wanted* British Intelligence to get hold of Soma-2."

"Quite so."

"Oh, but I left out about my trip to Chepton Vale," Apple said. He explained at length about Mavis Regland, the fire, her sickness. "Which reminds me. Is there any after-effect from the drug?"

Tibor nodded in that wonderful, understanding way he had. "Yes, a period of *katasak*. It begins a week after taking the drug and lasts one month."

"*Katasak*," Apple said. "What a pretty word."

"I do not have the time to explain now. I am sorry."

Apple rocked his head. "Please. It doesn't matter in the slightest. Nothing matters." He went on rocking because of the pleasant sensation of his head against a piece of grit.

Tibor asked, "What did you do upon realizing the point of our being with the circus?"

"Nothing. I went home. Here, that is. I was highly ashamed of myself for not having seen it earlier and fed up with Angus Watkin for not telling me. How silly I was to be upset."

"Are you sure Watkin knows?"

"Of course he does. Otherwise he wouldn't have sent amateur Appleton Porter in. That's all I am. A faceless one."

"I mean," Tibor said, "you did not contact him? You did not convey to him what you had learned?"

"No. He'd pull me out. Now that I know, you see, I might give it away to the KGB that we know what they're up to. That would be fatal."

"So possibly he does not think the way you do about the KGB wanting him to have the drug."

Anxious to oblige, Apple said, "It is possible, yes. Anything's possible with Angus Watkin."

Tibor smiled. "You do not like him, I think."

"I'm afraid that's true, Tibor."

"You may tell me why, if you wish."

Apple wished. He brought out every one of his complaints against his superior. He was having a wonderful time.

Tibor stated, "You do, however, like the Service."

"Mostly, yes. There are some aspects of it that disturb me, but I don't think about them. To me it's a game."

"A game, Apple?"

"That's right. And as far as I'm concerned, the name of the game is stalemate." He raised his head as a nod. "No one can win. Although, yes, it would be a fine thing if we of the West could release the satellite nations, Hungary included."

"You do not hate the Russians?"

"Heavens, no. They're great people. It's their government that's the problem. It won't let the people do what they want or go where they want. It's serfdom pretending to be an ideal. I could go on, but I don't want to bore you."

"And here you have freedom, you believe?"

"Relatively," Apple said. "And a rich relative at that. If a man doesn't like his job, he changes it. Or his town. Or his country."

"Yes," Tibor said quietly. "Yes."

"Yourself, for example. If you were fed up with working with animals, you could do something else. You could have a try at being anything you fancied."

"That is the way it used to be in Hungary. I have not been

back since I was a young man, but I know it is different now, the same as in Russia."

"How sad," Apple said, but with a smile.

Tibor leaned forward and clasped his hands. "Let me ask you some more questions."

The first thing Apple became aware of was a squeaking. It had a not unpleasant lack of pattern. He was reminded of small, furry animals, and that made a nice change from large ones.

Behind the squeaks was a rumbling. That became a bore, droning on as it did without breaks or highlights. It matched the tremble that Apple now realized was moving his whole body. That, and his discomfort, were also boring.

He opened his eyes. There was dimness. The cause was personal, not general: he lay under a cover of some kind. He could see the cracks of light at the edges from his awkward position on his side. The awkwardness came from his hands being behind him. He tried to change that and found that his wrists were tied.

Understanding came rapidly as Apple smelled the soil and recognised the sounds. He was in the back of his station wagon. What covered his head and shoulders was the leather windcheater. He was a prisoner, though his feet and legs were free. He was being driven somewhere.

Apple lay still. He thought back. The last thing he could recall was talking in his hotel room with Tibor, after having cleverly switched the cups of coffee.

With a leer of disgust, Apple realized that he had out-clevered himself. He had fallen for one of the oldest tricks in the book, as any good greenhorn would. He had switched the drugged drink onto himself. Soma-2, of course, was the answer. He could taste strawberries.

So by now, Apple thought, the KGB trio knew everything.

Most likely they had all been there in the hotel. He would have told them whatever they wanted to know, which had to mean that the mission was over, just as their game was over, blown by his knowledge of them wanting to plant the drug. Was his life over as well?

Cautiously, Apple began to work himself free of the windcheater. To see was to fear less. He shifted his head and twitched his upper shoulder, making no sound. Vaguely, he wondered why the car was being driven at what seemed a slow speed.

The windcheater eased backwards, helped by his body's trembling. In a minute he was able to get his nose under the edge; next, his whole face. He saw that he was being driven by Tibor Polk. There was no one else in the station wagon.

His windcheater fell right back and off. Tibor glanced around, looked again. He said, "Ah, you are awake."

Apple asked a cold, "What's going on?"

"You will see. First, I shall stop here for one small moment so that I can release you."

"Release me? Then why did you tie me up?"

The older man stopped the car, leaned back over the seat. "As a precaution," he said, reaching to Apple's wrists. "You might have attacked me, the way you did that jailer after you had awakened in the cell."

"I see I told you everything," Apple said, determined not to show that he was mystified. His hands came free.

"Everything. Please sit in the front. You may do the driving, if you wish."

Legs first, Apple slid over into the passenger seat. "That's all right."

Anxiously Tibor asked, as he sent the car forward, "You are not hurt? I was not driving too quickly?"

"I'm fine, thank you," Apple said, disarmed. "Kind of you to be so thoughtful."

"I have no wish to hurt you. You or anyone else."

"You know what I am, however."

"You are an operative of British Intelligence. I, though, am not a member of the KGB." He spun the steering wheel. They turned off the narrow country road onto a rough track that climbed across the centre of a field.

Apple asked, "Where are we going?"

"To a place where we can talk in peace. A ruined cottage. Anton, Tina, and I, we went there for a picnic the other day."

"They must be KGB, but it's not easy to believe in Tina's case. She doesn't look hard enough."

"Much harder than Anton. Both outside and in. She has no emotions, and in unarmed combat, she could tie him into small knots."

Apple looked openly at the driver. He could see, among the sadness and nervousness, a new aspect: determination.

"I don't understand this," Apple said. "Any of it. Why are we coming out here? We could've gone on talking at the hotel."

"The others might have arrived, interrupted."

The station wagon topped the rise. Into view came a cottage. Half the roof was gone, as were the windows and door. Nearby trees moved in the light wind like mourners.

"About the drug," Apple said. He wanted, without asking, to have it confirmed that he had given away that he knew what the game was.

"Which you call Soma-2," Tibor said. "You told me everything. It is all down on tape."

Apple sighed. "You certainly fooled me by getting me to switch the drugged coffee onto myself. It was neat."

Tibor shook his head as he brought the car to a halt by the

cottage. "I was not trying to fool you. I did nothing. I had simply put the drug in my own coffee. For me to drink."

Apple stared at him. "Do you know what you're saying?"

"Of course."

"You wanted to drug yourself?"

"Exactly, Apple. I hope you do not mind if I call you that. I did in the hotel. I think we are going to be friends."

"Well . . ."

Tibor said, "I sensed from the start that you had a sympathetic character. I did not believe that you were a spy. When it seemed certain that you were, refusing a drink in Tina's this morning, I was surprised. I began to think old thoughts in a new way."

"Yes?"

"But my decision came at the last minute. In the room. Until then, I had merely been following KGB instructions. Knowing that I lacked the courage to go through with my decision, I thought to give the drug to myself instead of to you. I wanted to be able to be honest."

The room smelt of decay and furtive meetings. Pock-marks and smears of dirt covered the walls between stretches of graffiti. Rubble and dead meals lay about the floor, which had islands of wooden boxes. The ruined cottage was as romantic as a letter from a bank.

Apple didn't care. He was too excited and engrossed to notice. He sat on a box, leaning forward, nodding encouragement to Tibor, who sat on another box right in front of him. Their heads were close together. They were on their third cigarette.

Tibor had been giving an outline of his life. Childhood, youth, and early manhood had been spent in Buda with his widowed mother. He became a chemist in a government laboratory and quickly made his mark. After the uprising of 1956, he was transferred to a post in Moscow. He was allowed to take his mother along. In time, he was given the task of working on an improved version of the so-called truth drugs. He was happy. A narcotic that would make people be perfectly honest with each other was exactly what the world needed, he thought, but thought secretly.

It hadn't been long before Tibor realized that the discovery he was closing in on would be used with less noble motives. But there was nothing he could do about it. If he failed he would be made to suffer in various ways, including loss of his comfortable flat, which meant that his mother would suffer most. If he refused outright, he would be certified as mentally ill and confined to an institution.

Tibor had worked on. He created the best drug yet in the field. Soon after that, he was included in a scheme designed by the KGB. With his mother left behind, he was sent to Paris. There, cover was established and the circus act perfected over a period of six months. Then the trio came to Britain.

"The reason I was permitted to go beyond the Iron Curtain is, of course, obvious," Tibor said.

"The invisible umbilical cord."

"She is old and unwell. I could never do anything to hurt her."

"The KGB feeling easy about letting you come to the West, that I can understand. But why did you have to come at all?"

"Someone had to pass himself off as the amateur dabbler in chemistry, the one who had discovered this drug. He would need to be able to discourse knowledgeably about his work, should British Intelligence send an expert to talk to him, that is me, the pro-Western animal-keeper. That was one reason."

Tibor put out his cigarette on the floor, but tidily. "Another," he said, "was because I had told the KGB that I wanted to test certain fruits and vegetables in Europe, relative to perfecting my antidote to what you call Soma-2. The first part of that was true, the second not."

Apple asked, "An antidote isn't possible?"

"Oh yes," Tibor said. "I have already found it."

"Oh."

He tapped the crown of his white hair. "It is in here. Where it will stay. Whatever my original creation is being used for at present, I am not going to give it an enemy."

"But the KGB are waiting for you to produce an antidote."

"Yes. I am supposed to be working on it constantly. There was a small laboratory in the trailer. Destroyed now. That would have given me some weeks of breathing space. It does not matter now."

Apple put out his cigarette. "It's because of the forthcoming antidote, then, that your bosses were eager to give this truth drug to the West."

"Yes. The country was unimportant, by the way. Britain was chosen because the circumstances were right."

"The idea would be for us to use Soma-2 on KGB agents, who had let themselves be worked into an accessible position. They would, of course, have taken the antidote beforehand."

"And be familiar with the behaviour of a person under the influence of Soma-2."

"So that we would accept every bit of information they gave us as gospel," Apple said. "Yes, it's neat. A trick like that is worth a lot of stage-dressing."

"I agree."

"But, Tibor, you know you will have to produce this antidote sooner or later."

"It does not matter now," the Hungarian said again, adding, "Nor that I am not going to make any more Soma-2."

"Why doesn't it matter?"

"Because," Tibor said quietly, "I want to stay in the West."

"You . . . ?"

"Yes, Apple. I want to stay here. I want to stop working on drugs. I want to be where I can do that. I want to do research in other directions. In fact, I want to do and be and say many things that are not possible in Russia."

Apple had an increase in his excitement. "You know what that means, staying in the West?"

"I do indeed. I have cogitated on it with care."

"It means, in a word, defection."

Tibor got up. He began to pace, hands deep in the pockets of his smock. "And, you are thinking, I cannot do that because of my old mother."

"It did occur to me, yes."

"I have, as I mentioned, cogitated on this matter with care. Great care. I believe I have the solution."

"Yes?"

"If I might have another cigarette, please. As you can see, I am not as calm as I might be."

Apple got up. He supplied cigarettes and used his lighter. Sitting again, drawing quickly at the smoke, he kept his eyes on Tibor, who continued to pace.

"The solution," Tibor said, "is for me to be kidnapped by the West."

"Seem to be, you mean?"

"Precisely. And which country seemed to do it, that could be left in doubt, so that there would be no international repercussions—not, at any rate, against any particular nation."

Apple said, "It would need to be done realistically."

106

"Quite so. Otherwise, all would be lost. My mother would suffer. If, however, the kidnapping was believed, she would be treated better than before."

"Better?"

"Yes, for I would be considered a hero."

Apple smiled. "Why, I believe you're right."

"I am convinced of it," Tibor said, pacing and smoking. "I know the mentality of the people I work under. They are always eager to build up a new martyr, a man of the people suffering in the name of Communism."

"That's true, Tibor."

"With my features rendered a little more noble, I might, in time, appear on a postage stamp." He smiled, became serious again, took several fast puffs on his cigarette. "So, Apple, I am going to ask a favour of you."

"Name it."

"I am going to ask that you get your organization to kidnap me. It will be a secret defection, but a public abduction, with frills and fanfare. Is that possible?"

"I believe so," Apple said, elated. He had been sent in to get a drug and would come out with its brilliant creator. "I can very soon find out."

"And when all the fuss has died down, I would like to find a job with some research laboratory. Is that also possible?"

"That's simple. You'll be able to take your pick."

Tossing his cigarette aside, as if it were a piece of chain, Tibor came and stood in front of Apple. He asked, "How long will it take you to find out if your people are willing to stage the imitation kidnapping? Two days? A week?"

"All I need is one telephone call."

Again the older man smiled. "Can it be that easy?"

"To get an answer, yes. How long the kidnapping itself will take to arrange, I don't know. It has to be done right."

"Yes—right. Perfect."

Apple got up. "Let's go."

He left Tibor in the car, which he had parked on a quiet street on the outskirts of Taunton. So as not to increase the other man's nervousness, he strode until he went around the first corner; then he broke into a run.

Rush, fool, he thought in glee. You're on to the biggest, fattest coup in the espionage game in years. What price a sympathetic nature now, Mr. Watkin, sir?

Coming to a telephone booth, Apple went in but kept the door ajar with his foot, as was his habit; he didn't like enclosed places if they were overly small. Being overheard was not a factor: It being lunchtime, the street was deserted.

Apple used all the coins he had, dialled the London area code, and the pertinent number. A man answered at once. Apple signalled urgency by saying, "I think I misdialled." He gave another number.

There was a short wait. The man said, "No, you were right the first time." Which meant that Angus Watkin was available.

"I'm in a public box," Apple said. "And short of change." He chanted more digits, reading them from the instrument he was using. "Got that?"

The man grunted, "Good-bye."

Putting down the receiver, Apple waited. He told himself to remember to ask Tibor about the drug, whether or not it had an after-effect, which would save him needing to call the doctor in Chepton Vale.

Even though Apple was staring at the telephone, his nerves

seared him as it rang. He let three more rings pass, airily, before lifting the receiver. He said, "Good day, sir."

"I trust this is genuinely urgent, Porter," Angus Watkin said. "Being the knight courageous at a fire doesn't bestow any special privileges on you."

"I'm aware of that, sir," Apple said. "This really is priority stuff." He wasn't in the least surprised to hear that his superior knew about the trailer fire. Only the reverse would have surprised him.

"Very well," Watkin said. "Please be brief."

"First of all," Apple lied, "I quickly realized that the group were KGB, not genuine showpeople. Or anyway, the two young ones were. I next realized that you knew about that as well as the fact that they were trying to get you to take the drug. In other words, I had been sent in on a Fools-rush." He mused: Go on, say you're going to pull me out, that my knowledge has made me useless. Please.

Watkin said a cruel, calm, "Good for you, Porter. But that is hardly the reason you called in. I did ask you to be brief, I believe."

Recovering from being cheated out of a crow, Apple went on to tell of his morning, ending with the recent talk with Tibor. "Polk's a brilliant chemist, as you know, sir," he said. "And he wants to come over to us."

Angus Watkin drawled, "Oh, really?"

Apple told himself he should have known better than to expect enthusiasm and gratitude. But he seemed to sense the former in Watkin's responses as he outlined the plan.

"That's possible, isn't it, sir?"

"Physically, yes. Nothing could be simpler. But think of the storm it would raise, even though we make it look like a foreign operation. Moscow would, I imagine, buy that. They'd assume us to be too sensible to do such a thing on our own doorstep. But think of the fuss over us letting it happen at all. There would be questions in the House, letters of apology at high levels. Think of that, Porter."

"Well, yes. It could be a bit messy."

Angus Watkin sprung his little trap. "Although, on second view, Moscow wouldn't be able to say a word because this Polk has nothing to do with them. He's supposed to be a French citizen."

You childish, smug-faced bastard, Apple fumed. He tried a snappy, "That had occurred to me."

As if unhearing, Watkin went on, "On the other hand, knowing the Russians, they'd claim that the papers were phony (which they are), that some kind of impersonation was going on, that Tibor Polk was on holiday in the West. What's more, they would be able to prove it. They would raise all manner of stink in trying to get their man back."

Apple gave in. He sagged against the glass wall. Weakly he asked, "Then it's no go?"

"What?"

"This kidnapping."

"Oh, yes," Angus Watkin said briskly. "We'll arrange for that."

Apple sagged still further while producing a feeble grin. Quickly he straightened. "Very good, sir. When?" But you didn't ask questions of Angus Watkin, whose answer was:

"The tape that was taken in the hotel room. You know what to do about that, naturally."

"Yes, sir," Apple said. "We scrub it out and make a new one, with me admitting to being an agent but not mentioning about knowing this is a set-up. I'll say how useful this drug will be, once we've got hold of it. We'll use it on the rotten bloody Reds, I'll say. I'll lay it on nicely."

"You will do nothing of the kind, Porter. You will not be so obvious. These are not idiots you are dealing with, you know."

Seething dislike for his superior kept Apple from blushing. He mumbled, "No, sir."

Watkin said, "What you will do, Porter, when making out a new tape with Polk, is confess that you are not really a market gardener. You're an animal trainer. You have realized that they use some trick in the control of their animals, probably some kind of soporific, and you want to buy it. That, I believe, will keep them in bliss."

"I think you're right, sir."

"They will brush you aside and wait for the next approach."

Apple nodded, then blinked. I'm about to be pulled out, he thought. This is it. I ought to have kept my mouth shut about knowing what Upstairs knows. It's all over.

Angus Watkin asked, "Are you there?"

Apple took a deep, settling breath. "Yes, sir," he said. "I was just waving to Polk, who's in the car."

"I see."

"He gets upset if he loses sight of me for long. As far as he's concerned, everything hinges on me."

A drawled, "Is that so?"

"Yes, sir. Quite, sir."

"Good-bye, Porter," Watkin said. "I'll be in touch with you." The line went dead.

Apple put down the receiver slowly. He presumed that he was, for the moment, still in. But either way, all credit for bringing home a star defector would be his, and there was nothing that Watkin could do about it.

Apple left the telephone booth. The street was still quiet. He went to the corner, around it and toward the station wagon. Smiling, he waved. The door opened and Tibor got out. Apple told him as he hurried the last few yards, "Yes. It's being arranged. It could happen anytime."

"Thank you," the Hungarian said. He sagged and gave a tired smile. "Thank you very much."

They shook hands and patted each other on the shoulder. It came to Apple, gratefully, that he had never been looked at in quite this way before, as if he were a saviour or miracle worker, or the staunchest of friends. If he got no other reward, he thought, this would be something to remember.

Clearing his throat, Apple brought out cigarettes. "The next step," he said, "is the tape." He began to explain.

Tibor listened while patting his pockets. Slowly, his face drew on an expression of shock.

The tyres screamed as the station wagon zoomed around another corner. They had hardly stopped complaining from the last. Bodywork squeaks, those small furry animals, made a constant twittering; it seemed to Apple to be like the clamour of his nerve ends.

"I am so absent-minded," Tibor mumbled. He was hunched inside his smock and clinging to the door handle.

Grimly: "Nothing to worry about."

"I had forgotten all about the recorder until you mentioned it just now. I do not think I even switched it off."

"It'll still be there," Apple said, twisting the steering wheel again. The car squeaked and screamed as it bore around the bend. Suburbs almost over, they were nearing the centre of town.

Tibor said, "I am seriously troubled. We have been such a

long time. Anton or Tina could have gone to the hotel to investigate."

"But would they go in the room?"

"Without a moment's hesitation. And to them, any lock is a toy."

"We haven't been all that long."

Tibor asked, swaying as the car hurtled around a traffic island, "You understand what it means, if they play the tape?"

Apple nodded. "They'll know the game's up, that they've been twigged. They'll skip out at once—before your abduction can be arranged."

"In the room you said you had not told your superiors that you knew what was going on. Anton and Tina might decide to risk that only you yourself have guessed the truth. Which means that you would have to be removed. Silenced."

"Oh."

"But no," Tibor said. "It will not come to that. I am the one in trouble—if the tape is played."

"Why's that?"

"I spoke in such a way that it will be very obvious that I have defection in mind. In my enthusiasm I forgot the existence of the recorder. I asked you many questions about life here, while making derogatory statements about the Soviet Union."

"I wish you'd told me this before," Apple said. He shot out onto a main road without pausing to check the traffic. The road was clear. "But never mind."

"To the KGB I am more important than this particular scheme," the older man said. He ran a hand fretfully over his hair. "They can always try it in another country."

"That's true."

"So they will leave even faster than if simply knowing the game is up. And, of course, I will be made to go with them."

"You could always just escape."

Tibor said, "For my mother's sake, it has to be an abduction or nothing."

Apple took the car around another corner. He arrived on a downtown street. With anguish, he saw that it was crowded. Lunchtime was ending. The pavements were thick with people —shoppers, office workers returning to the job, staff going back to the stores. Traffic was slow and heavy.

Apple cursed his decision to cut through the middle of town rather than circle suburbs to reach Wintertree. Mournfully he braked on coming up behind a delivery van. The bodywork fell silent, but he still seemed to hear the squeaking from his nerves.

"You must hurry," Tibor fretted. "Please."

"I'm trying, I'm trying."

The other lanes were dense with cars. Passing was out of the question. Apple cut back to the inside. A side street appeared. To get into it, he drove over the corner of the pavement. An outraged woman hit the car with her umbrella.

The street was clear. Apple put his foot flat to the floor after changing up into second gear. The station wagon responded well. Soon they were hitting fifty. Apple prayed that he wouldn't get lost.

Spurting and braking, taking straight runs and dozens of bends, he went along street after street. He saw no landmarks. Logic told him to stop and ask directions, emotion refused to let him waste the time needed to do so.

"Hurry," Tibor repeated, rocking back and forth. His hair was awry from worried scufflings.

Apple turned the car onto yet another road. His heart jerked when he saw the hotel. It was right in front of him. He sped over, parked untidily, and leapt out.

With Tibor close behind, Apple ran inside, into the deserted lobby. He grabbed his key from its pigeonhole, raced to the stairs, went up. He had unlocked the door and was pushing it open by the time Tibor arrived, panting. They went in.

"Oh God," the older man said.

"It's gone?"

"It was on that table."

They stared at the table's empty top. Apple grasped at, "The room's been tidied. Look, the bed's made." He hustled around, crashing open drawers and cupboards and the clothes closet. He found nothing.

Tibor said again, "Oh God."

Apple thought of Jimmy. He snapped, "Come on."

They hurried down to the lobby. Tibor let himself slump into a chair while Apple strode along a passage. He stopped and stepped back after passing an open doorway. In the small room, a maid was folding linen. He asked her if she had seen anything of a tape recorder in room twenty-six. She said she hadn't. Only two coffee cups.

Apple went on. He found gap-tooth Jimmy in the kitchen, making himself a pancake. Performing a greasy smile, Apple asked, "You didn't by any chance borrow my tape recorder, did you, Jimmy?" Steal, is what he meant; steal for the collection of show biz memorabilia.

The youth's denial was genuine, Apple could see. He asked if anyone else might have been likely to go in his room. Jimmy said, "Not that I know of, Mr. Porter."

The bearer of sick news, Apple went slowly as he returned to the lobby. It was empty. No Tibor. Frowning, Apple looked in the dining room, checked the washroom. He called the Hungarian's name. That only brought Jimmy, his mother, and the maid. Apple ignored their looks and went outside.

The station wagon was gone.

Apple ran at full speed along the street. He was heading out of town. People stopped to stare, moved well aside as he flashed by, gave shouts of encouragement.

By now, if he were in London, Apple knew he would have seen a score of taxis. Here they didn't exist, not as a roving enterprise. There were only chauffeured hire-cars, available at once but only from the office.

So that's what he should look for, Apple told himself for the second time, instead of running like an idiot. As before, he ignored the advice of logic and went haring toward the Bridgwater Road. He knew of only one place to try to find Tibor: the showground.

The street he was on had a trickle of traffic. At every rumble of approach from behind, Apple semi-turned and stuck out his thumb. He was either ignored or treated to a derisive blast on the horn.

Apple ran on.

Tibor, he knew, would not have gone off in the station wagon. Not without a word. He was the type of man who would be well mannered even when terrified. So he must have been taken away by the other two, who must therefore have heard the tape.

Hissing at himself, Apple realized that Tina and Anton had probably been keeping a watch on the hotel. They had seen the departure of himself and Tibor, had gone in and taken the recorder. Later, during the chat to Jimmy, they had spirited Tibor out of the lobby. All they wanted to do now, was get their defection-minded chemist out of the country.

Apple turned onto the Bridgwater Road. His lungs were heaving. Each gasp was hard, painful work. His arms were spinning like wheels in the edges of his vision. His feet kept up a rapid drumming.

Apple was glad to know that he was more concerned about Tibor than himself. A feather in his Service cap was all he would fail to gain, while Tibor, he would lose everything, with the possibility of being incarcerated as a certified lunatic or sent to Siberia.

The traffic was heavier here, but no more mindful of giving rides. Other hitch-hikers sat or walked along the roadside. Apple gave up moving his thumbing arm out of its helpful rhythm.

Thankful for his long legs, he ran at full power. He knew quite well that he couldn't keep up this pace long enough to carry him to the circus, some three miles out, but that didn't make any difference. He went on running.

The traffic thickened, slowing as it did. Apple kept on glancing behind. He passed two cyclists and a put-putting wheelchair. Every time his feet pounded down he got a shock of pain in the top of his skull. The dive-bomber damage was being revived.

On his next glance back, Apple saw a truck lumbering along. Old, it had a running-board. As it drew closer he moved out into the roadway. His backglancing became a rapid to and fro.

The truck came level. Apple charged at it, leapt, landed on the running-board safely. But then he felt himself being thrown backwards. He flung out both arms. One hand managed to grab the extended rear-view mirror, the other went through the open window and slammed against the cab's roof.

A voice snarled, "What the bloody hell . . . ?"

Apple drew himself back. He put his head inside the cab and, while trying to get enough breath to speak, made urgent eyes at the driver. His head and shoulders bowed rapidly. His mouth gaped for air.

Looking torn between anxiety and anger, the driver said, "Don't try to speak yet." He was young, beefy, with a Skinhead haircut and a razor scar down one bulky cheek. A cigarette bobbed between his lips.

Apple gasped, "It's . . . it's . . ."

"Wait," the driver said past his cigarette. "Hold on till you can breathe, mate, for Christ's sake."

"It's . . . I must . . ."

"Hold on. Wait a bit."

Apple went on bowing, but slower. He was recovering fast. He panted, "I've got to . . ."

"You can tell me the emergency in a minute," the driver said. He glared a piteous warning, shook his head, breathed in quickly to demonstrate. He drew in too much smoke from his cigarette. He began to cough.

"Don't try . . ." he started, choking.

Apple shook his head and gasped, "Wait."

"Hold on . . ."

"I must . . . wait . . . don't."

The driver, red-faced, staring, coughed on in short heaves, spittle flying past the cigarette. He oozed out, "Don't try talk."

Apple swallowed. He panted, "Wait a bit. Get your breath."

The driver said, "Take it easy." He was winning the fight with his lungs. Tears came from his eyes.

With a surge of cheer, Apple saw that they were almost at the showground. He yelled, "Stop!"

Shuddering, his mouth a wide slit of panic, the driver slammed on the brakes. His truck slowed with a grinding noise. While that was still going on, Apple jumped off. He was dead level with the gate. He ran toward it, throwing back a wave of thanks when the driver shouted:

"What's the emergency?"

The fairground attractions were open for the pre-matinée trade. Apple charged up the centre of the midway, through the light scattering of early customers. His breathing was erratic, but bearable. He gave more waves, answering calls from operators, among them Amelia Earhart.

He turned into the maze. With fair certainty he made his way toward the twin trailers, which he found. There, he stopped with a rush. The last thing he had expected was a crowd.

There were twenty or thirty of the circus people standing under or around Tina's awning. They were partly or fully changed into their performance clothes. Talk faded away as they all turned to look at Apple.

He asked, "What's going on?"

A dwarf said, "That is exactly what we'd like to know." His tone was accusing.

Nick Stick pushed through to the front. "The Hungarians have taken off in a hurry," he said. He was in his clown get-up, all except the bulbous red nose. His attitude was no more friendly than the other clown's.

"Why did they take off?"

Frowning, strong-man Arvo said, "We do not know." Oddly, he wore jeans under his leopard skin. "They came rushing back, ran in and out of the trailer, throwing things around, and then left."

Apple nodded. "I see."

"They left, Mr. Porter, in your car."

Apple gazed around. Belligerence showed on every face. He said, "I'm as mystified as you are. My car was taken from outside my hotel. I got a lift out here."

Nick Stick said, "You've been seeing a lot of these three. I reckon you know what this is all about." He took a step forward. The others did the same. They had an air of menace.

Apple took a stride to the rear. "I don't know a thing."

Arvo pointed out, "But you are obviously very agitated, Mr. Porter. Even your breathing is affected."

"I've been running."

Everyone moved another step forward as the dwarf grated, "You just said you got a lift."

Apple didn't have time to argue. He turned and ran.

At once, Apple went into a dead-end; a box formed by vehicles. On quickly reaching the mouth again, he came face to face with the pursuing crowd. He slipped aside and into another grass-floored alley. Yelling, the crowd gave chase.

The happening had a nightmare quality. So much so that Apple had to laugh in order not to feel unnerved. A look back showed him the waving, shouting stream of people, most in weird dress, led by a clown. He ran as fast as the maze would allow.

Coming out on the midway, Apple was turning toward the gate when he heard a loud grumbling. He swung around, went the other way. The mob was close behind. Everyone else stopped to gape.

Two greasy youths were by the Wall of Death, each astride a flashy but cheap motorcycle, which was being revved as an attention-getter. Because of the noise, neither youth heard the clamour.

Apple ran to the nearest bike. He grabbed its handlebar with one hand while using the other to shove its rider. The youth was knocked off. He went staggering away.

Apple swung into the saddle. He didn't like motorcycles, never rode them, but had been taught their use in Training Eight. He gave throttle and moved away. As he did so, the crowd arrived, and Nick Stick's hand slid off Apple's shoulder.

People scattered at the sight of the motorcycle. They leapt

aside and dragged children through the air. Apple was trailed by curses as he bumped along the midway. He reached the gate, passed through onto the road. He shot off, quickly picking up speed. He would have felt elated if he hadn't been worried about Tibor.

At a junction, Apple looked back. There was nothing in view except another motorcyclist. It was not the second youth from the Wall of Death, but a man in full cycling rig. Apple felt safe in respect of what lay behind.

But he didn't reduce speed. He went far above the limit as he curved onto a lesser road that would take him around the town. After curving, he looked back again. The other motorcyclist was still there, and gaining. He had a leather jacket, helmet, goggles . . .

Apple turned his head front and speeded up. The other rider wasn't a he, but a she. It was Amelia Earhart.

He had to lose her quickly, Apple thought. Although he could handle a lone woman with ease, it could be awkward if she followed him right to the ruined cottage, which was the only place he could think of where the trio might have gone.

However, as Apple raced on, glances back showed him that Amelia was losing no ground. The motorcycles would be alike, he realized, therefore equal in power. He wasn't going to be caught—unless the fuel ran out—but neither was he going to leave the other machine behind.

Presently Apple reached another junction. He swung onto a third-class road, hard on top but decrepit. It had holes in the surface as big as heads. Hitting one of these, he nearly came off. He raced on along a weaving course.

Usefully, the road began to bend. Most of the time, Amelia Earhart was out of sight. Apple scanned the way ahead keenly.

He was looking for a place, maybe a farmyard, into which he could dodge and hide.

A better idea came when he saw, over the tall hedges, the top of a van. It was approaching. He slowed. The van, for furniture removal, drew abreast and went by. Apple glanced back. Amelia wasn't yet in view. Making a sharp U-turn, scraping his shoe on the road, Apple shot at top speed after the van. Reaching it, he cut in between the body and the hedge. He stayed there.

Seconds later, looking behind, he saw Amelia Earhart. She was going the other way, bent determinedly over the handlebars.

Apple let the van draw ahead. He passed it on the correct side and went back to the junction. Within ten minutes, he was on another country road. Two minutes after that, he reached the field he had driven across with Tibor.

Cutting his motor, Apple coasted into the field. He turned away and footed to the hedge, where he left the motorcycle. He set off up the rough track. When the roof of the ruined cottage poked into view above the hill's crest, he lowered his head. He went in a cautious crouch until he could see all the cottage and its surrounds. The station wagon was not there.

Apple sighed. That was it. He had no more ideas. And possibly this had been a poor one to begin with. The Hammer and Sickle could be on their way to London, with Tibor a virtual prisoner.

Was there a chance, Apple wondered, of the station wagon being parked around the other side of the cottage? He admitted, without hope, that there was. He thought he might as well look, so long as he was here.

Retreating until he had only the roof in sight, Apple circled the field. When far enough around, not using caution, he climbed. He saw walls, trees—and a car's roof. He strode up swiftly. The car was the station wagon.

Apple ran on up. It was as if he were ascending to get level with his heart, which felt high in his chest. He became careful on drawing closer. Stooping, he kept the car between himself and the cottage. There looked to be about fifteen feet separating the two.

The final stretch Apple covered on all-fours. He stayed in a squat after reaching the side of the station wagon. He listened. There was a voice. A man was speaking. Apple listened with greater concentration. He recognised the voice as his own.

The tape was being played.

Raising himself, Apple looked through the double stretch of glass. The sound was coming from the nearest window gap. Through it, he could see nothing. He raised himself higher, then higher, then higher yet, until he was looking over the car's top.

As Apple straightened still more, in the room a shape began to appear. It looked like a mammoth brown egg. Anton Gavor, Apple thought, sinking swiftly.

He crawled along to the front and again started his circumspect rising. His taped voice was telling about Mavis Regland and the fire. When Apple was easing himself up above the hood, he saw white hair. For the moment, having located Tibor, that would do. He squatted.

At length, the tape ended. Inside the cottage a discussion in Russian started as to what had been said. Anton was firm, Tibor defensive and querulous. He kept saying, "Your interpretation is wrong, comrade."

"We do not think so, comrade."

"You see dangers everywhere and in nothing."

Anton said, "Your feelings are quite explicit on that tape, as you must know. Why are you attempting this absurd denial?"

"I've told you and told you," Tibor said wearily. "I was leading the subject on, trying for more information. I am familiar with the phases of the drug, but perhaps you think you know more about it than I do."

"Save your speeches, comrade. Our superiors will deal with this."

Tibor began huffing that their superiors would be dealing with comrades Gavor and Koves, who were making a grave error. Apple rose swiftly. He went to his total six feet seven inches so that he was in full view of the white-haired Hungarian. Tibor saw him and stopped talking in mid-sentence. Apple squatted again.

Anton asked testily, "What's wrong with you?"

After a faltering start, Tibor said that he was only now realizing the vast and terrible enormity of the mistake that was being made. "I am shocked."

"You cannot possibly be more shocked than I am, comrade. Though perhaps I shouldn't use that term of honour with you."

"What utter nonsense."

Apple tensed. From somewhere behind him he had heard a stealthy sound. He waited. The sound came again. Quickly he jerked his head around. As he did so, a rabbit popped into sight from a clump of grass. It went bounding away. Involuntarily, Apple let out a laugh of release. He clamped a hand to his mouth, hearing Anton say:

"What was that? Did you hear something?"

"No," Tina said. "What was it?"

When the shaven-headed man spoke again, his voice was closer. Apple knew that he had come to the window. Anton said, "It's only a rabbit."

"You are a trifle nervous, comrade."

"That is a matter of opinion," Anton Gavor said coldly, his

voice fading as he left the window. "Personally, I believe I have myself and the situation well in hand."

"*We* have it in hand," Tina said.

Still cold: "I beg your pardon, comrade."

"When you two have finished," Tibor said, "I would like to point out that in the near future you might not be so eager to claim authorship of this absurdity."

Tina laughed. "I grant you full marks for trying."

In a loud, carrying voice, Tibor went on, "You have come to an insane conclusion. It was madness of you to desert the circus. If you were convinced that the British secret service know what this Porter simpleton has guessed, by a fluke, about the plan for the drug, then you should have eased out of the situation gradually, not decamped under strange circumstances."

"We do not need advice," Anton said.

Tibor persisted, "It was madness of you to make that telephone call to London, to our Embassy, and ask them to send reenforcements. That's making a mountain of this ant-heap. You could so easily have driven there."

"In a known vehicle?" Tina asked. "And be stopped within ten minutes?"

So, Apple thought as the argument went on, the Russians were sending help. That could mean anytime. Now, tonight, tomorrow. Once they arrived, Tibor was finished.

With no particular plan in mind, only the need for a means of flight, Apple crept to the car door. He turned the handle, pulled. The door came open with a faint squeal. The trio went on talking. Apple looked inside the station wagon. The ignition had no key. They would not, he told himself, have been stupid enough to leave it in.

Rising midway, Apple put his upper body into the car. He reached under the steering column to the wires there. It took him only a few seconds to separate the pair that worked the ignition. He broke them free, pushed them up out of sight. When he was easing himself back down out of the car he heard Tina ask, her voice clear:

"Anton, did you leave the car door open?"

The man with the shaven head replied, "I don't think so. Would it be a mistake if I had? Quite inexcusable?"

"You had better check it."

"Oh well," Anton said in a bored tone. "All right."

Apple looked all around swiftly. He saw only the open field, going down to a line of trees, which were hundreds of yards away. In any case, Tina, he sensed, was still watching from the window. The only hope seemed to be underneath the car.

Apple lay down, stretching himself flat. The station wagon was low. When he tried to roll beneath it, his shoulders caught on the frame. He could hear the scuffle in the grass of approaching footsteps. As he pushed away and sat up, Anton came into view and saw him.

Shouting, the Hammer ran forward. Apple shot to his feet. He and Anton collided. They bounced off from the meeting.

Anton Gavor spun, recovered, turned. His face was grim. With less haste now, he came forward again. He came in the unarmed combat crouch. His hands were flat for chopping.

Apple's mind took him back eight years to his training at Damian House. But then, as the other man rushed in, he went further back, instinct beating training; back to his schooldays, when, needing to fight in answer to the ridicule being thrown at him on account of his height, he had been given boxing lessons by his father.

Apple did a Marquis of Queensberry. He jerked erect, poised his right, and held out a straight left.

Anton stopped his rush. He blinked a mixture of surprise and suspicion. He blinked again as a long arm tapped a punch on his nose. The karate chops he countered with met only air; he wasn't close enough; that long left was keeping him back. He went on blinking.

Apple was still trying to order himself to stop this schoolboy nonsense, when he threw a tremendous right-hander. It connected with Anton's jaw. The Hammer cried out and went careening backwards. He began to fall. His head hit the car's front bumper with a resounding clang. He slumped to the ground. He lay still. His eyes were closed.

Apple roared with pain. The blow out of nowhere, coming in silence, had landed on his left kidney.

Falling to the grass, Apple rolled. In flashes during the rolling, which he kept up to ease the pain and form a defence, he saw Tina. She was stalking after him, hands out and sliced. Tibor stood worriedly in the background.

Groaning, Apple got up. He was still undecided about which pose to take, old or new, when he was amazed to see Tina leave the ground. She rose up horizontal and came at him feet first. Her slip-ons crashed against his brow. He went staggering.

"Help!" Tibor shouted. "We are being attacked by this English madman! Somebody help!"

Purblinded by tears of pain, Apple managed to keep his balance. But Tina, in jeans and shirt, was flying through the air at him again. He was able to dodge just far enough so that the feet went by, but the rest of the Sickle smashed into him obliquely. They went down together in a heap.

Tibor was going on with his camouflage shouting. Anton Gavor began to groan.

Too close for effective work, Apple and Tina slapped and grappled. It was like wrestling with a child, Apple felt. He gave a tremendous shove. With Tina rolling away, he leapt up and ran toward Anton, pulling the belt free from his jeans while he went.

Apple reached the Hammer, whom he needed to keep out of the action. He turned him onto his face. That was as far as he got. Tina was back. She threw a kick that landed on Apple's chest. It had been meant for his face, but his face was much higher than normal.

Deciding to stay with success, never mind what the rules said, Apple threw out a stylish left. It went over the top of the Sickle's head. She was much smaller than normal. She came in under the arm to give him a chop to the side of his neck.

Apple weaved away, groggy. He went on staggering backwards as Tina came after him. She was smiling.

"Help!" Tibor shouted. He was standing over Anton with a rock in his hand. He made as though to bring it down on the egglike head, but hesitated.

"That's right!" Apple yelled. "That's the way!" He hoped Tina wouldn't understand and look around. He told her in a lower voice, "That's the way, my girl."

Tibor tried again, shook his head, dropped the rock aside.

Apple realized he was still holding his belt. With a sudden movement he brought it whistling over and down. The strip of leather lashed across Tina's face. Apple winced. A red mark had appeared even before the girl, screeching, shot up both hands.

Apple ran back to Anton. Quickly he put the Hammer's arms behind him and bound them at the wrist with his belt. This time he followed the prescribed method. Tibor came up and hissed, "Push me." Apple obliged. The older man stumbled backwards and sat down. He again called for help.

Apple bent back to work. Before he could get Anton Gavor's own belt unbuckled, Tina came racing back into action. She was no longer smiling. A livid red line lay across her face.

Aiming lower, Apple shot out his left. It was grabbed in two hands. He felt himself being lifted, obeying an awesome pain in his shoulder. He left the ground and flew through space. The ride seemed to last for minutes. Finally he landed in a bone-crunching slam against the grass. He groaned. He felt unable to get up.

A shoe skimmed past his cheek. He raised his arms. The next kick he deflected, the third he turned to his own advantage. He grabbed the ankle and twisted. Tina yelped and lost her balance. Apple wearily rose.

He loped back toward Anton. He wasn't fast enough. Even limping, Tina soon caught up. Turning flabbily, Apple put out a staying arm. The Sickle reached for his wrist.

"That's it, comrade!" Tibor shouted, appearing suddenly between them. "We'll overpower the swine together!" He tripped, fell heavily against Tina and knocked her down. He landed on top of her.

Apple went on. With the other two shouting at each other, one in rage, one in apology, he unfastened Anton's belt and zip, pulled his riding britches down past the red-striped underwear and gathered them around his boots. Drawing the tongue end of the belt out, he wrapped it around a second time before slipping it through the buckle. Damian House would have been proud.

Straightening, Apple turned. He was a mass of aches and pains. The other two had got free of the entanglement. They were rising. Tibor was saying how they could overpower the madman spy. Tina snapped, "Stay out of it, you useless old grandfather."

She, Tibor, and Apple moved toward a no-man's land. They stopped at the clatter. As the noise grew, they exchanged questioning glances. Then their heads shot up as the helicopter appeared.

Plain black, without markings, the helicopter wooshed abruptly into view above the cottage, its racket tripling in volume. It was a large machine with a cabin behind the pilot's bubble.

Apple began to back away. He felt double-beaten. Nevertheless, he gave a mental nod of admiration to the Russians for their prompt response to the call for re-enforcements.

The helicopter had circled. Now it began to come down some distance away, on level ground beyond the cottage.

With a yell of triumph, Tina ran forward. She called back, "Come on, comrade. Bring Anton."

Tibor looked at Apple. He was sagging in resignation. He said, "It was a nice dream but now it is over. I must go, and so must you."

Apple nodded. "Yes," he said. "Good-bye, Tibor."

"Good-bye, my friend."

Apple moved toward the station wagon. Half-way there, he halted on seeing that Tina had changed direction. She was now hurrying back from the helicopter, which had almost reached the ground. Its cabin door was open. In the doorway stood a figure.

Tina's face showed fear.

She reached the car, snatched open the door. "Quick!" she shouted to Tibor. "Get Anton in." Seeing there was no key in the ignition, she ran to the man on the ground and began trying to find his pockets in the concertina of riding britches.

Apple was staring at the helicopter's doorway. The man there, bracing himself, was small and middle-aged. He wore white sneakers and a blue coverall.

"My God," Apple whispered. "It's Albert."

Stunned and delighted, Apple went on staring. He told himself he ought to have known better than to be fooled by Angus

Watkin's cool reaction to the news of a brilliant defector. This was a highly important affair.

Tina had the key. "Leave Anton!" she ordered. "Get in the car!" She got in herself. The starter whirled uselessly.

Apple rushed at Tibor. He grabbed him. "We're saved," he said. "Struggle." The older man performed so readily and violently that he tore himself loose. Apple grabbed him back.

The helicopter touched down at the same time as Tina ran from the nonstarting car. She charged at Apple and Tibor, did a magnificent hand-spring, and in arising from that shot up into the air. Her feet came straight at Apple's head, and hit.

He fell and rolled. When he sat up, Tina was already some yards away, running down the sloping field, towing Tibor behind her and snarling at him to hurry.

Apple got up. Without haste, for show, he followed. He had had enough of the rough stuff. The rest of it he would leave to the others. Stopping, he looked back.

Two people were running in a crouch from the helicopter. They were heading toward the station wagon. The first person was Albert. The second was Amelia Earhart.

Apple smiled at that even as he was wondering, But why are they going . . . ?

Albert and Amelia stopped beside Anton. With one taking his feet, the other his shoulders, they lifted him up and carried him off. They went toward the helicopter.

Apple mumbled, "Hey." Dumbfounded, he watched for a moment; then started to run. He charged up the slope. "Stop!" he shouted, even though he knew nothing could be heard that close to the helicopter's racket.

The carrying pair reached the doorway. They bundled Anton inside. The machine was already rising as they got in themselves.

It had zoomed up to fifty feet before Apple reached the spot. He halted, sagged, gazed around.

Tina had ended her escape. She and Tibor were looking up at the helicopter. Bewildered, Apple did the same. They watched until the black aircraft had faded from sight. The silence was immense.

Limply, Tina and Tibor came up the slope at a plod. The chemist looked at Apple, his eyes begging for an explanation or an assurance. Apple turned his head as he started ambling back. He had nothing to offer. He hadn't a clue. The only solution that occurred to him was that Angus Watkin had lost his mind.

The trio stopped within yards of each other. They formed a stupefied triangle. The first to recover was Tina. In English she said, "Polk and I are leaving. If you try to stop us, I shall hurt you. This time I will be serious."

"I believe you."

"Now. What have you done to the car?"

"Find out."

She came a step closer. "I can make you tell me."

Apple said, "I didn't do anything. It's an old model. It gets that way at times."

All three people twitched at a new sound. It was a blast on a car horn. It came from somewhere on the other side of the building.

Apple ran. This, he thought, must be the solution. Tina ran with him. Together they circled the cottage and stopped to look down the other side of the hill. Coming up the rough track were a pair of grey limousines.

Tina ran on down toward the cars. She waved and called a greeting. The language she used was Russian.

Apple turned. He charged in the other direction. He met

Tibor, who had been following, grasped his shoulder and swung him around, kept a hold and pulled him along.

Urgently he said, "They're here. The KGB re-enforcements that were sent for. Let's move."

"Move?"

"We've got to leave."

"But how can I go like this?" Tibor wailed, still running. "It is not possible."

"It is if you do what I tell you."

Two minutes later, Apple was semi-lying across the station wagon's front seat, keeping out of sight. He had already connected the ignition wires. Tibor was crouching on the floor of the passenger side.

There came the sound of cars' engines. Not until they stopped, along with an order in Russian to search the house, did Apple reach to the starter button; and not until doors were slamming did he press it in.

The motor sprang to life as he shot up straight, in position behind the steering wheel. At the same time, Tibor got off the floor, kneeled on the seat, and put his upper body through the window.

He yelled, "Help! Save me! Help!"

There were seven or eight men, all short and broad and in dark suits. They erupted into shouts and action. Some ran at the car as Apple sent it surging forward, and continued to chase on foot. Others, with Tina, hurried back into the limousines.

"Help me!" Tibor bellowed.

Apple sent the station wagon hurtling down the slope. Bouncing, thrilled, he said to Tibor, "That'll do for the moment. Come inside and hold on."

The chemist complied. His face was flushed, his eyes were

sparkling. As he landed back on the seat from a huge bounce he said, "You are a genius."

Apple said, "Oh, I don't know." He glanced in the rear-view mirror. The runners had given up. The first car was just moving off. "In any case, this is only to give us a respite. The real pretend abduction has to come later."

"But why? I acted very well."

"But will Moscow be convinced of your innocence? Remember the tape. What you need to do now is escape from me and call the Embassy. Ask for help, you, a loyal son of Moscow."

"Yes, I see what you mean."

"We'll go into it later."

Tibor asked, "And why did that helicopter take Anton?"

"That's something else we'll go into later."

They reached the trees, which were set well apart. Apple drove between trunks. He went as fast as he dared. He said:

"The trick now is to keep you safely away from both the Russians and the British. My chief would accept this as show enough. He wouldn't think about your mother."

"I am in your hands, my friend."

They came out of the trees onto a lane. Apple went along it quickly. Far sooner than expected, the first limousine burst into sight behind. The other came next.

Apple put his foot flat to the floor. His elation slackened as he thought of the lane running into a dead-end farmyard. But he told himself that things had gone too well for this to finish up so stupidly. Fate wouldn't be so unkind.

Tibor stated, "You are worried."

"No, not at all." He looked in the rear-view mirror. The big grey car was gaining. In one more minute it would be bashing at the rear bumper.

Ahead lay a gateway. Beyond that, right beside the lane, stood a haystack. It was the stack's outward teeter that drew Apple's attention. He smiled.

"Hold on," he said as he sped through the gate. When almost level with the stack, he wrenched the steering wheel around and then swiftly back again. The car swiped against the haystack and went on.

Apple looked back. Hay was falling. It seemed to be doing so in slow motion; too slow to be any good. But as the first limousine came abreast of that point, a load came down neatly onto the hood, blinding the windshield. The car stopped.

"A genius," Tibor said. He put his head out of the window to bellow an exuberant, "Help!"

Call it three minutes, Apple thought. It might do, as long as they didn't run out of lane.

There was another gateway, another haystack. Through the mirror Apple checked that the cars were not in sight. After going through the gate he spun the wheel mightily. The station wagon skidded, took hold, turned off the track. Apple steered behind the stack and halted with a jolt.

He and Tibor sat quietly. The wait was achingly long to Apple's racing nerves. But then the roar of motors grew; grew and then faded.

CHAPTER 4

"When you make the first call to the Russian Embassy, act very agitated. Tell them you've given me the slip, but that I can't be far away. You're in a public box, tell them. It's on the Wellington Road going out of Taunton—that's nicely on the other side from here—and would they come and get you at once."

"Yes, I see."

"On the next call, maybe an hour later, tell them you had to run from there. Men came after you. They were foreigners, you think, not English. Make that clear."

"I shall."

"Possibly, you say, all the telephones in the area have been bugged, and this call could be being listened to now. So you won't say where you are, to be on the safe side. You tell them you'll meet them somewhere in London."

"They will ask me to go to the Embassy."

"You won't listen. You're distraught. And you won't be expected to think of that yourself because you're not the type. You're an absent-minded professor."

"Then where in London do I tell them to meet me?"

"I'm working on that."

Apple and Tibor were walking along a winding country road. It was quiet. Trees formed a canopy overhead, which is why the road had been opted for rather than open country: They wouldn't be seen by a helicopter. For the same reason, the sta-

137

tion wagon had been abandoned under a large, spreading oak.

Here, Apple felt safe. In the quietness, approaching vehicles could be heard long before they appeared. That allowed time enough for getting over the low hedge and out of sight. Already it had happened twice; first as a tractor went by, second when one of the Wall of Death's greasy youths came along on a motorcycle, his eyes carefully scanning the landscape.

"So you'll be drawing them off our tracks," Apple said, "as well as establishing your loyalty to Mother Russia."

"Brilliant, my friend."

"And don't forget to lay on that loyalty with a heavy hand. A lot depends on it."

"Rely on me," Tibor said. Having discarded the smock, he wore a crumpled worsted suit. It matched the old Tibor Polk of sadness, not the one who was now striding along with shoulders back and head held high.

He said, "I shall weep for a glimpse of the Kremlin."

"I shouldn't go that far, Tibor."

"If you say so. I'll sniffle."

Abruptly, Apple grabbed the older man and brought them both to a stop. Leaning forward, he said, "Listen."

"Yes, it's a car."

They ran to the hedge. Apple cleared it with a leap, Tibor threw himself over as if diving into a pool. On the grass they crouched down. Apple peered through onto the road. The car, being driven at an easy pace, held two men. Youngish, they wore sports shirts and sat in comfortable sprawls.

The car went by. Apple got up and drew Tibor with him, saying, "British Intelligence."

"You know them?"

"No, but they have the right amount of casualness, as if they were going to fall asleep in a minute."

"Wait," Tibor hissed. "Another one."

They shot down again, only just in time: the car, coming from the same direction, was going at speed. Peering, Apple got a glimpse of a large grey limousine.

Tibor said, "The countryside is rife with seekers."

"And with more being called in all the time," Apple said, "if I know anything."

"Which you do."

They returned to the road. Apple went on being content, in spite of the fact that his body ached in every part. He felt like a seasoned operative, an old hand, a real pro.

The Hungarian asked, "May I have another cigarette, please?"

"All gone. But there's a town ahead. I'll get some there and buy the other things you need. Come on, let's step it out."

Arms swinging, they marched. The sun speckled them with rays through the foliage, Tibor whistled, Apple thought he wouldn't mind going on forever like this. A mission was afoot, success lay ahead. This was what the game was all about.

Twice more over the following ten minutes they had to break off, get behind the hedge, when farmers in trucks came along. Or, as the older man pointed out, what seemed to be farmers.

The canopy of trees ended. Buildings began to appear. Apple and Tibor left the road. Awkwardly, going cross-current, they made their way over a ploughed field. The next was easy—a meadow lying fallow.

They began to run, for the fun and freedom of it. And then they began to run in earnest as the chattering, battering sound came floating over the air.

Glancing up and around, his head twisting urgently for first sight of the helicopter, Apple ran with one hand gripping Tibor's shoulder. He was pushing the Hungarian in front of him, hissing, "Faster, faster."

They had changed course, were aiming for the only available cover. Ahead stood a tree. One tree. It was small, with the minimum of foliage, but it would have to do.

The racket was growing louder as they arrived at the slim trunk. Apple saw at once that the bowl of foliage was too small for cover, except for directly above. He stooped to grab Tibor's legs, gasping, "Up you go."

Lifted, Tibor grasped a branch. He started to pull himself up. Apple sped a look around and saw the helicopter appear over near-distant buildings. It was dark green.

He leapt for a branch of his own, dragged himself up onto it, reached down and helped Tibor make it into deeper cover. They sat holding onto each other and panting.

The clatter grew. It swelled to an ear-offending bedlam. The leaves went mad, grass all around started to dance, Apple held on grimly to Tibor and the branch.

The noise wound down. Stooping, Apple watched from under the foliage as the helicopter floated away over the skyline. He bulged his cheeks with a breath of relief.

"All clear?" Tibor asked.

"Yes, but we'll hang on a bit in case they sweep back—a standard trick. In fact, you can wait here while I go into town. This is as good a hiding place as any. Okay?"

"Okay."

The 'copter's colour told nothing, Apple thought. The searchers could have been anybody. There might have been a clue if the letters and numbers on the side had been readable, but they hadn't, not from that angle.

Apple was in a vegetable garden, which he took as a good

sign: the aptness, considering his cover story. There were other long stretches of garden on either hand. They led to the backs of buildings, houses of two or three stories.

Apple walked upright and openly. He had nothing to fear here, save as a trespasser. The danger lay in being on streets and roads, where any of the seekers might spot him. He had no more wish to run into the British than the KGB. Watkin would demand to have the chemist, whom he was not going to have until the scene had been perfectly set and the act carried out.

The garden led to a lawn. Beyond that was a truck-sized heap of beer crates. Next, in a yard right beside the building, were brick outhouses with doors marked *Yer Tis*. The place was a pub. Apple told himself that he had known the garden was a good sign.

He was able to stroll into a crowded room, slouching to lower his height, and have no one give him more than a passing glance. He himself swept faces and types carefully before he stopped at the bar. There, burly men were drinking pints of cider. To the barman Apple gave his order, whispering because of the effete-seeming sherry on the rocks.

"We got no rocks," the barman said loudly. Talk at the bar took a rest. "If you mean ice."

Apple winced and sagged lower at the knees. He hissed, "Yes, but it doesn't matter."

"Oi mean, zur, this ain't the Ritz nor even the Savoy," the barman said. "Ice?"

"I don't want ice really," Apple mumbled. "Straight. Just give it to me as it comes."

"Sweet or dry?" the barman asked loudly. "Ice, he wanted."

Apple said, "Dry, please." He added hurriedly, to forestall another question, "Any brand will do."

The barman grunted, the drinkers went back to their talk and cider. Apple felt able to straighten himself fully. On doing so, he caught sight of his face in a mirror. He stared.

There was a lump on one brow the size of half an egg, on the other a ripe purple bruise. He had a graze on his left cheek, which was also smeared with dirt. Blood was encrusted around his nostrils and one corner of his mouth, near where there was another bruise. His shirt collar was torn, his jacket filthy.

That was one thing not taken into account by the people responsible for Training Four, Apple thought. It wasn't necessarily the actor who created the attention; more often it was the audience. Obviously, he had chosen the right kind of pub.

Feeling progressively more the old pro, Apple paid for his sherry. At the same time he bought matches and four packets of cigarettes, which he stowed in his pockets. He knocked the drink back in a gulp, turned away, and headed for the rear of the room.

Outside, he took off his leather jacket and slapped it free of dirt; or anyway to an acceptable degree of dirtiness. Jacket on again, he went into the washroom. There was one muck-encrusted sink and one corner left of a mirror.

Soapless, Apple washed, with many ouches at the hurt. His reflection had improved. He looked at himself with narrowed eyes for a moment, rather taken by the tough-guy image, before lighting a needed cigarette and going out.

Head down, he passed through the pub. He came out on a narrow, winding street. Traffic was light, though the pavements were busy. There was nothing to be seen worthy of causing alarm.

Apple asked an old woman. Following her directions he went to a corner and along another street of the same type. There were business places all along the way. Ahead was a four-way

junction, with a policeman on point duty. He was mostly direct-
ing pedal bikes.

Before that, Apple came to the shop. It sold used clothing. Inside, Apple was served by a small woman who, despite the heat,
had a fur piece around her neck. She was able to supply a blue
raincoat, but could offer nothing in the way of headgear. "People 'ave a thing against second-'and 'ats," she said. "It's been the
curse of me life."

With the coat over his shoulder, Apple went out. He began to
retrace his steps, knowing he had passed several places on the
way where he could buy a cap.

He scanned people keenly. All was clear. He glanced behind—
and saw Nick Stick. Apple swung fully around, moved to the inside of the pavement, sagged and lifted the raincoat to part-
cover his face. He started moving backwards.

He hadn't been seen by the clown, who was at the junction,
leaning on a corner, gazing around as if in boredom. He looked
this way. Apple stopped. Nick Stick held the direction of his
gaze. He frowned and scratched his ear.

Just then, a man went up to him. They spoke. Apple used the
diversion to go on back and into the recessed doorway of a shop.
He peeked out with caution. Now there were two men talking
to Nick Stick, who was shaking his head.

Seekers, Apple thought. Anyone tall is a suspect.

"What you up to?" a voice asked. "Want something?"

Apple turned. He was being stared at crossly by a man in an
alpaca jacket. The shop was a haberdashery. Apple walked past
the man briskly.

"Thank you, yes," he said. "A cap."

Throughout the transaction, he was watched warily by the
man, for he refused to turn away from his position facing the
door. The cap he examined by bringing it up near his face, and

paid for by thrusting the money aside. No one passed in the street.

Leaving cautiously, Apple saw that the men had gone and that Nick Stick was strolling off in the other direction, still looking bored. Apple strode away.

Five minutes later, via the pub, he was arriving at the tree. He called, "Come on down, Tibor."

There was no answer. Apple went beneath the branches and stared up. There was no one in the foliage. Apple groaned and looked around. He saw the Hungarian immediately. He was in a corner of the meadow, picking daisies and dandelions.

Apple shouted. Tibor started. Guiltily he put the flowers down and came trotting across. He said, "Just filling time." He could have passed for ten years younger than he had looked this morning.

He put on the coat, pocketed the matches and cigarettes, watched with compassion as Apple scuffed the cap against the tree trunk to remove its look of newness, absently wiped it with his sleeve before putting it on. Apple tugged the peak down to the eyebrows.

"Obliterate the brow and hairline," he quoted. "The second most recognisable area of a face after the eyes." He was surprised himself at the difference.

"It is a fine cap," Tibor said. "Thank you."

"Don't take it off," Apple warned. He went on with other advice while handing Tibor money, and on one of the notes jotting down his Bloomsbury telephone number. That he was a seasoned operator was now almost a conviction.

"Stay away from roads. Keep going in this same northeasterly direction for at least two hours, until you're well clear of this sector. Then get a bus or a hire-car. Understand?"

"Perfectly, but . . ."

"If you should happen to be caught in open country by a chopper, a helicopter, don't run. Stare up at it, like anyone else would. Cup both hands around your eyes and look fascinated."

"Yes, but . . ."

"Make that first telephone call to the KGB as soon as possible, and keep it brief. Pant and panic. Sound as if you're scared to death. Understand?"

"Yes," Tibor said. "But why are you telling me all this? I shall be with you."

Apple shook his head. "We're splitting up. We would never make it together. My height's too much of a giveaway. You'll manage fine on your own. But stay away from roads for the time being."

Resigned, Tibor asked, "Where will we meet again?"

"Paddington Station," Apple said. "In London."

"I know of it."

"At eight o'clock tonight."

"Very well."

"And that's the information I want you to give the KGB when you make the last call to them. That will be their rendezvous place with you, as you supposedly return to the fold."

"I understand," Tibor said. "And so we must part for now, my friend."

"Until eight at Paddington."

They shook hands. About to move off, Apple said, "By the way, Tibor. I've been meaning to ask you. Is there a delayed after-effect with Soma-2?"

As the Hungarian nodded, he looked like a boy at fault. "Well, yes," he said sheepishly. "A mere inconvenience. Nothing permanent."

"What is it?"

"Well, thirst," Tibor said, settling his cap. "Starting about a

145

week after taking the drug, lasting for a month, there'll be a thirst that you feel you cannot quench. Sorry."

"I think I can stand that," Apple said. He backed away. "See you later, Tibor."

For half an hour, after circling the small town, Apple himself went across country in a northeasterly direction, though at a different angle from the one that Tibor would be taking. Sometimes he used roads. He had less fear of being spotted now that he was away from the chemist.

At one junction, Apple had seen a car standing. A young couple inside were in each other's arms, but not kissing. They didn't kiss during the five minutes that Apple watched, from cover. He liked neither that nor the fact of their being parked in full view —hardly a lovers' gambit. He gave the junction a wide berth.

He had done the same five minutes later when seeing at a crossing a truck parked by the hedge. The two roughly dressed men in the cab were pretending to look at a map.

Now Apple was approaching another cross-roads. This one also had a stationary car. Its front was up and a girl was half-hidden inside the engine. She wore jeans and a T-shirt. Her hips were particularly shapely.

Apple went ahead. Reaching the car he asked, "Can I help?" His smile changed from polite to real as the girl withdrew and stood erect. She was five feet ten inches tall at the very least and in moccasins at that.

She smiled back, saying, "Thank God."

Her hair was dark and wavy, reaching her shoulders. About twenty-five, she had an attractive, strong-featured face and beautiful teeth. Her eyes were brown, large, expressive. What they told was unusual joy as she went on:

"Thank God I was the one to find you, Apple."

146

He blinked. Forgetting his plan of asking for a lift, in exchange for fixing the car, he took a closer look. He nodded. Dully he said, "Amelia Earhart."

"At your service," the girl said. "Hello." She stuck out her hand. "Jane's my real name."

Apple gave the hand an unenthusiastic shake. "Well, goodbye."

"Not likely," the girl said. "Not after me spending an hour in and out from under this bloody lid." Her smile grew. "And to think, it was me who scored."

A faceless one, Apple thought. Maybe her very first time out in the field. Speciality: knowledge of fairgrounds and familiarity with the travelling showpeople.

He suggested the latter. Jane nodded, saying, "And guess what. The circus is my first mission."

"Then why aren't you there now?"

"I closed up my joint. I said there was a fault with the motor." She drew him around to the car's passenger side and opened the door. "By the way, sorry again about your terrible ride. I think I understand now how it was done."

"Don't bother to explain," Apple said. "It's sure to be over my head." He allowed himself to be ushered inside.

Jane closed the door, closed the front and strode gracefully around to the other side. She slipped in behind the wheel. "First," she said, "off this road. Agreed?"

"Agreed."

It took her one minute to start up, reverse, back into a gateway and swing around behind a shed. Apple decided he couldn't have done better himself. He looked the girl up and down with interest and respectable lust.

"Second," Jane said. "Where is he?"

"Ah, well, that's a tricky question."

"If you can't tell me, tell Angus Watkin. You have to call in. That's an order."

Apple got out cigarettes, which he offered. When they were both smoking, he asked, "Why was Anton lifted?"

"I'm not sure I'm supposed to tell you, as you surely must realize. I'm under need-to-know."

Not liking himself, Apple said, "I'm not sure I'm going to stay in this car."

"He was lifted," Jane said, "because of a mistake."

"I like that."

"It seems that Upstairs suspected camouflage. They thought that tough-egg Anton could really be the chemist, and the older, sensitive type could be the Hammer."

"Neat thinking."

"But wrong."

"So it was blamed on Upstairs," Apple said. "When the guesses go right, old Angus gets the credit."

Jane blew out smoke. "Anyway, when Albert saw Anton tied up, that was the clincher. We didn't have room for anyone else. And when we went back the place was deserted."

"Where's Anton now?"

"I really have no idea. I was dumped. Later, I was told to help look for you and Tibor Polk." She tossed her hair back. "I'm glad I always liked Tibor."

"Did you know what the set-up was?"

"No. Except for maybe Anton, I thought they were straight. You as well. I was only brought in on this today. I still don't know much about it, but I dare say it goes back to the pop bottle I sent Upstairs."

Avoiding the hint, Apple asked, "What's happening at the scene of the hasty flight?"

"The showground?" Jane said. "Well, everything's neat. The

twin trailers were rented, so that's no problem. The RSPCA is going to take the gorillas. The story to explain that fast exit by the trio is that they're burglars. You, a past victim, were closing in. Is it tidy enough for you, sir?"

"Without a doubt."

"Good," Jane said. "Now you have to call in."

Apple nodded slowly while putting out his cigarette in the ashtray. "I didn't want to do that until later." He looked up. "Let's go and have a drink."

Sprightly: "Dare we?"

"Damn right we dare. If you're sure I'm not a Hammer."

"Don't," Jane said, starting the motor. "I tend to believe what I'm told. Possibly that's why they don't use me very often."

"And possibly it's because missions with fairs don't happen every other day," Apple soothed.

"Mmm. You'd better get out of sight." When he had squeezed himself down onto the floor in a tight squat, the car moved off. Jane said:

"I suppose you're on missions all the time."

He mumbled around that and into, "Do you know you have a charming nose?" He was too ego-high to be embarrassed at his nerve in giving a girl a compliment.

"Oh, I have not."

"Yes, you have." He put his elbow on the seat, his hand under his chin, and gazed up at the driver.

She said, "Stop staring at me."

"You're worth a stare or two."

Jane blushed.

My God, she's blushing, Apple told himself, and thought she could even be as much as five-eleven.

149

They stopped on the parking area behind a small, ancient, isolated inn. There were two other vehicles, both manure-laden trucks. It was late, close to the three o'clock closing time.

Apple and Jane went in by the back way. They clumped along a flagstone passage. Apple went into the snug, a small room with stuffed fish and monks' benches, while Jane went on in search of the bar. Soon she came back with two sherries on the rocks.

"Thought I'd try one myself," she said. "It's clean out there, by the way."

They sat on a bench, sipped their drinks, smoked, and talked. Jane told of her work of keeping an eye on the Chinese jugglers, though without going into details. Her biggest problem, she said, was holding Sir Jasper in line. He had been told of the situation, in order to get Amelia Earhart established on the scene, and he wanted to play spy.

Apple was liking Jane more by the minute. That went up by one step when she asked how tall he was, another when she brought back from the washroom a soapy handkerchief, with which she proceeded to clean the grazes on his cheeks. Her touch was gentle. So was the movement of her unfettered breasts against the T-shirt.

"Last orders!" a voice called sonorously, like a nightwatchman telling what o'clock it was. "Last orders, please!"

When Jane returned with fresh drinks, she said, "The landlord, from page two of Pickwick Papers, says we can stay as long as we like, as far as he's concerned."

"Sit down," Apple said. "Listen."

Skipping mention of drugs and plots for placing same, Apple told the personal side of the story—Tibor's need for a kidnapping show, in order to protect his mother. He ended:

"I have to keep him away from Watkin until a really good scene's been set."

"Poor Tibor," Jane said.

"To answer your question of where is he, he's footing it out of here, aiming for London."

"I don't know if he'll make it. We've got roadblocks set up all over the place."

"He'll be staying away from roads," Apple said. "But how do I explain not holding onto him?"

Jane shook her head. "I don't know. But if you don't call in, and it's found out afterwards that I gave you the order to do so, then you'll be up the creek."

And, Apple thought, you won't get any credit for being the one who had found Appleton Porter. He liked her more for the fact that she hadn't said it.

"You'll need Watkin's help anyway," Jane pointed out. "For the imitation snatch."

"Only in respect of manpower. This is my game. I'm setting the scene." He wondered if Tibor's admiration of him had gone to his head, or if it was the respectful look in Jane's eyes, or if it could be the sherry.

He got up abruptly. "I'll call in."

Like a hollow monster, a dark and stuffy telephone booth lurked around a corner of the passage. Apple had to use his lighter to see what he was doing. It didn't make him feel any better that, needing to be prudent, he kept the door closed.

He snapped off his lighter when a voice over the wire droned, "Yes, you dialled the right number." The next speaker was Angus Watkin, who said a lordly:

"Took you long enough, Porter."

"Yes, sir. There've been problems."

"No doubt."

"One being that Tibor Polk isn't with me now. We separated. I was forced to let him go."

Where anyone else would have screamed with rage, Watkin sounded faintly peeved. "You let him go, mm?"

"Had to, sir," Apple said, "to prove to him that I was genuine. To prove, you see, that I wasn't trying to pull some kind of fast one. But we've set a meeting for later."

"What, Porter, is a fast one?"

Apple said, "After some terrible mistake had been made, the wrong man being picked up by our helicopter, Mr. Polk stopped trusting me. If I hadn't let him go, he would've given me the slip. But it'll all turn out fine."

"How jolly."

"I mean, he'll turn up tonight."

"Which will be where and when, Porter?"

"Paddington Station at eight. The KGB will be there as well, so they'll be able to see the kidnapping. Mr. Polk will have told them by now, as per my instructions."

There was a long silence. It ended by Angus Watkin asking a heavy, drawled, lethal, "*Your* instructions?"

In a bustle Apple said, "Yes, sir, but he's vaguely disguised, so he'll be safe enough until he's in our hands, then we let people see who he is, and also there should be only Tina there who knows him well, unless Anton shows up, which I suppose he could, couldn't he, this being a free country."

"Anton Gavor," Watkin said, as if in spite of himself, "is in hospital. He was rescued from a lonely farmhouse by police helicopter, with a broken leg."

"His leg wasn't broken."

"It is now."

Apple repressed a shudder. "Yes, sir," he said. "So you see, there'll only be one KGB at Paddington who knows Tibor."

"But rather a lot who know you, Porter."

"Me, sir?"

"In any case, all this is unnecessary. A scene is not on. You have done your—er—best, Porter, and I shall speak to you about it on another occasion. That is all."

"All, sir?"

Angus Watkin said, "I'm pulling you out."

There was a short pause. Apple said loudly, "Hello? Can you hear me? I'm afraid you've faded away, sir. Hello? You were saying something about a scene. Hello?"

"I can hear you perfectly well," Watkin said.

"What? It's coming and going, getting stronger and then fainter. Hello, hello?"

"Listen to me, Porter. You are out of it. Do not under any circumstances show up at Paddington Station, for as you may just possibly realize . . ."

"Can you hear me?" Apple shouted. "You've gone completely now." He dabbled the cradle, making the line click. "There you are. No, that's someone else. It's getting worse. But I'll keep talking in case you can hear me at your end of . . ." He disconnected by putting the receiver down.

He went limp. Damp with sweat, he fumbled out of the gloomy booth. All his aches and pains were pushing for attention. He went back to the snug and sat with a slump beside Jane, who asked:

"Well? Did you lay down the law?"

"He tried to pull me out."

"You?"

Apple smiled sheepishly. He shook his head in denial and apology. "I'm not a full-time operative."

"You're not?"

He said, "This is only my second real mission." He perked, delighted, when Jane, far from bringing down a curtain, patted his arm and smiled.

"Whichever," she said, "you've done a marvellous job. And think of all you've been through. My God. That dive-bomber ride, the fight you had today."

"It's not only today."

"Oh, I'm sure it isn't."

When Apple had finished telling casually about his experience with the gorillas, he got out cigarettes. Accepting a light, Jane asked what was going to happen now.

"I'm staying in," Apple said. He explained about the phony lack of communication on the telephone. "I'm going to London and be at Paddington at eight."

"Is that wise?"

"Of course not. But I set this up. Furthermore, I was in it at the beginning."

"What does that mean?"

Apple said, "Angus Watkin invented an unwritten law about that, the starter having to be in at the kill. I'm going to take him up on it." He didn't go on to mention Fools-rush, which was the reason for Watkin's invention.

"Getting to London," Jane said. "That might not be so simple."

"The roadblocks?"

"Right. Watkin will pass the word, and you'll be taken into polite custody."

Apple sat up straight. He lifted his glass, drained it, set it down firmly. "If Tibor can do it, anyone can."

Jane asked, "But can he?"

"Yes. He'll do the corny, childish things that no one would suspect. He'll get through."

"I hope so."

Apple stood up. "Well, I suppose I'd better be moving."

Jane also got to her feet. The relationship in their heights was pleasant, Apple thought. Tossing her hair back, Jane said, "For the sake of Tibor's mother, I'll try to get you around old Watkin's blockade. I think I know a way."

Squeezed down on the floor at the passenger side, Apple exchanged background data with Jane, who drove swiftly and well. Their talk she interrupted occasionally to say, apropos of a passing car, "That's KGB," or, "That's got to be us."

In spite of his cramped, aching body, Apple was enjoying himself. He was smitten, for one thing. For another, it felt good to be able to talk with someone who was in the same line of work and roughly on the same level as himself. He bragged mildly about his first mission.

Jane began to tell of hers at the circus. She broke off to say, "This is where we turn off from civilization. Sorry about the bumps. We're leaving the road."

The car began to sway and bounce. Had he been by himself, Apple would have yelled at the assault on his sore muscles. Instead, he gritted his teeth in a grin and did some silent moaning. Jane kept glancing at him in sympathy. Once she patted his head.

The bumpy ride ended. Once again the car was speeding smoothly. Jane said with a sigh, "That's it, Apple. We've come through all the roadblocks."

"Thanks a million."

"If Watkin ever finds out . . ."

"I'll die first," Apple said. "I'd have to be hung, drawn, and quartered, and lose my pension."

"Don't exaggerate."

"Is it safe to get up now?"

"Yes, I think so."

He struggled up and onto the seat, where he sagged in luxury and gazed out at the busy highway. "But don't overdo it," he said. "You can drop me anywhere."

Jane said, "Another half hour won't make any difference, to anyone. I might as well drive you into Shaftesbury. You can get a taxi from there."

"You're great, Jane. Really."

They exchanged a smile. After clearing her throat, Jane went back to telling about the circus mission. It had had its moments of fun and interest and excitement, she said, and the only really tedious parts had been when she had needed to flirt with Nick Stick.

"That bloody clown of a clown," Apple said, bristling, jealous. "Why did you need to do that?"

"To try and find out his game. He's not straight, we're sure of it, but we don't know who he's working for—if anyone. Could be he's free-lancing for someone."

"So there could be others who are also interested in your team of jugglers."

"Who might turn out to be innocent," Jane said. "But Nick Stick, I think myself, personally, that he's possibly a Hammer, put there to watch the Hungarian trio but maybe without them knowing anything about it."

"Could very well be—Tibor's a pretty hot property. Another guard would be a smart move."

"And Nick was the one who mainly stirred the circus people's dislike of the trio, which meant they were left pretty well alone, to do as they wanted."

"All-round neat," Apple said. "But your flirting days are over. At least, as far as Nick Stick's concerned. He'll be drawn off now." He smirked with satisfaction. Jane caught his eye. They both smiled, then laughed.

The ride continued.

By the time they were coming into Shaftesbury, Apple felt as if he had known Jane for years, even though he only possessed her first name and couldn't ask for the rest. While eager to get on with the mission, he was sorry when the car stopped.

He said, "Well."

"Yes—well."

They looked at each other. Apple said, "I don't imagine we'll meet again. Unless it's in the line of duty."

"I dare say you're right."

"It's against the rules."

"I know," Jane said. "And they're probably sensible, all things considered. This is a pretty weird racket."

Apple sighed. He opened the door and got out, leaned back inside and again gave Jane his thanks for her help. "Believe me, I'll never forget it."

They shook hands. The hold lingered. Good-byes passed back and forth. Apple let go at last, quickly retreated, and closed the door. He strode off without looking back.

An hour later, after a fast ride, Apple was letting himself into his Bloomsbury apartment. All the way in the hire-car he had thought about Jane.

The flat had large rooms with high ceilings and was furnished in pseudo-Edwardian. It looked pompous to Apple after being away for days in a totally different world. But his fondness for the place made him be forgiving.

Even so, he destroyed the tidiness by flinging his jacket onto the floor and kicking a shoe into a corner as he went along to the bathroom. After setting the bath to filling with hot water, he strode to his living room and picked up the telephone.

Directory Enquiries got him the number of Wintertree. He called it and spoke with the proprietress. He arranged to have his bag sent on—when payment for the room had arrived. "I'll mail you a cheque," Apple said. "Give my best to Jimmy."

Disconnecting, he looked at his watch. It showed just after five o'clock. He told himself he had plenty of time; but he still strode as he returned to the bathroom.

Steeped in the hot water, Apple's muscles throbbed their thanks. He became dreamy with relief and comfort. To make sure he didn't fall asleep, which he often did at the best and fittest of times, he held one arm in the air. When it grew tired, he didn't lower it until the other arm had been sent aloft.

Apple had a long soak. Dried, he put on his tartan robe. The foot-square plaid leered in harsh reds and bile green. He glanced down at it admiringly while shaving with his electric razor. Last, he examined his face.

The half-egg lump had gone down, but the bruises were flourishing and the grazes livid and the puffiness still there. His eyes were surrounded by dark shadows. All in all, Apple mused, he looked either harrowed or sick.

Snapping his fingers, he went back to the telephone. He put a call through to Chepton Vale. He told the doctor that thirst was probably Mavis's problem. "It is," the doctor said. "Before and after the fact. Her illness is nothing more or less than a cracking hangover." Ringing off, Apple made a note to stick to water when the Soma-2 after-effect took hold.

He went into the kitchen. So that he wouldn't be startled by the pop-up, he watched the electric toaster after loading it with bread. He wondered what Jane was doing now.

Toast safely up, Apple made tea. He sat at the table with his snack. The toast he thinly buttered, thickly spread with lemon marmalade. He crunched happily. He got his thoughts in order.

Apple's jaw slowed and then stopped its chewing. It had occurred to him that things could be awkward, or worse, if he were to be seen at Paddington. The KGB would immediately assume a double-cross on Tibor's part. They would know, afterwards, that the snatch had been phony. They would also know, from knowing him, that it had been worked by the British. That, of course, was what Angus Watkin had meant by saying he had to stay away from the station, what he had been about to point out when cut off.

Apple blushed. Because it was deserved, his stupidity a stunner, he pictured himself in a mild sauna and without a fur coat, and he also left the door ajar.

His blushing cooled. He swallowed the mouthful of toast and ate on. The danger was obvious, he mused. Never mind the aftermath. He or Tibor could get hurt, and more likely the chemist than himself. But he was determined to be there.

What I need, Apple thought, is a disguise.

And, he further thought, how do you disguise a man who's six feet seven inches tall?

Apple ate on, crunching busily, eyes grim, until he found the answer. It came on the last slice, when he had been thinking that he might have to make more toast.

His satisfaction turned to alarm. He had remembered the time.

Looking at his watch, Apple realized that by now all the shops would be closed. Except, he told himself as he jumped up, crashing the table, in certain areas out of the West End. The nearest was Queensway.

Apple was sockless and still buttoning his shirt as he left the flat. He ran downstairs and out to the street. Being rush hour, he knew that a vacant taxi would be impossible to find.

He saw one at once. Hailing it, he got in and gave the direction, adding, "The fastest drivers get the biggest tips."

The cabbie, a middle-aged man, turned his head to the side. "And the biggest dents when they run into buses."

"Well," Apple said, winding down, "do your best."

He sat on the edge of the seat throughout the slow, stop-start, crawl-and-spurt journey to Marble Arch and along Bayswater Road. It would have been quicker to run, Apple thought; if he'd had enough energy. He got tired of looking at his watch.

Apple had the cabbie drop him at Queensway's end. He tipped well, skipped through traffic and went along the street of shops. Foreign influence was heavy here. A dozen traditions floated in the aromas that came from cafés, a dozen languages were catered for by the newsstands, a dozen ethnic types showed in the passing crowd.

Apple came to a sporting goods store. Inside, he went straight to a rack of track suits. They were blue with white lines down the sides. At the rack's very end he found a suit that would fit him. He took it to the counter and asked for a skiing cap. Shown a drawerful, he chose one in flaming scarlet with a fist-size bobble on top.

While waiting for his change, dithering one leg, Apple looked with regret at a ski hood with eye, nose, and mouth holes. It would be perfect if it weren't for the fact that hiding his face would draw attention.

He went out with his package, strode along to a shoestore. Footwear lay in racks outside. Seeing nothing there suitable, he went in. A Sikh in a turban came over. Apple asked for high-heel boots with zips at the sides.

"Outa fashion, int they," the Sikh said in a Cockney accent. "Six or seven years ago, they was big. But I fink we got a few in the back. What size you take, mate?"

Five minutes later, Apple was paying for a pair of brown

boots whose heels were five inches high. They would make him a nice even seven feet tall.

He left the shop and went back to the first, where he bought four basketballs and a net to carry them in. His last stop was in a pharmacy. He didn't care about the girl clerk's amused manner as he asked for a tube of pale lipstick.

Shopping over, Apple hurried across to the Underground station. He would shorten the trip back by taking a train to Tottenham Court Road, and running from there to home.

Still panting, Apple took off his jeans. They smelled, he now noticed, of grass, cars, beer, market gardens, burnt wood, sherry, sunbathing cream, and gorillas. He was passingly sad at the idea that sooner or later they would have to be washed.

Apple put on the boots. He tried a walk, which he had forgone in the shoestore because of haste. Although the zipped sides held his ankles firm, he was as wobbly as a toddler and moved in a forward-leaning, clumping gait like someone carrying a load.

It only needs a little practice, he told himself.

The telephone rang. Apple was clumping toward the instrument until he realized that the caller could be the friendly enemy. Angus Watkin, suspecting him to have left the Taunton area, might be trying to track him down, the motive containment.

Apple stood still until the ringing stopped. Sitting, he began drawing the track suit pants over his boots, which the stretch quality of the blue material permitted. Everything was fine, he saw, once he had the pants on, except that the cuffs' understraps allowed the high heels to be seen.

Apple thought about it.

While doing so, he prowled the flat to practice walking. He

improved. His stoop and clump became slightly less pro-nounced.

He found the answer on seeing, in the bathroom, a discarded sock. He went to his wardrobe and got a pair of stockings from a drawer. The telephone rang.

Watkin, Apple felt, wouldn't be trying again so soon. But that didn't mean it couldn't be Watkin this time, whereas it hadn't been before. He shrugged. He could never resist a call sig-nal anyway.

Clumping through to the living room Apple picked up the receiver. He recited his number in a gruff voice. Someone at the other end of the line whispered:

"Is Mr. Porter there, please?"

"No. Sorry."

"Who are you?"

"The landlord. I'm checking that everything's okay."

The someone asked, still whispering, "When do you expect Mr. Porter to return, please?"

It was the accent that Apple recognised. He said, "Tibor!"

They had a short, hurried talk. The Hungarian was near Lon-don, he reported. He had been chased by a bull but rescued by a farmer, who had driven him to a town, where he had caught the first of a series of buses. He had just landed in Uxbridge. He in-tended catching a train that arrived at Paddington Station at eight o'clock.

"Isn't that perfect, my friend?"

Apple hoped so, but with British Rail you never knew. "Yes," he said. "I'm proud of you." Their talk ended with Apple advis-ing Tibor to stay unobtrusive at the station until he, Apple, came to him.

Before leaving the telephone table, Apple looked in the book and jotted down numbers. He went back to his wardrobe. The socks he formed into a hard ball, which he wedged up between heel and curving sole of his boot. With the understrap over the socks, the pants leg was drawn tightly down. The heel was hidden and the cuff kept the ball in place.

While making this same arrangement on his other boot, Apple assured himself that everything with Tibor would go smoothly. The snatch couldn't fail. Although the KGB would be there, they would be greatly outnumbered by people from the Service.

Apple returned to the telephone. He dialled a number that he chose from those he had jotted down. A male voice answered, "London Lofty Lads here." It was a club for tall men that Apple had once been invited to join. He assumed a Welsh accent to say:

"Good evening. I think you ought to know that the Giants' League of Cardiff will be arriving at Paddington this evening at eight. They would appreciate it greatly, I know, if they were to be welcomed to London by some of your members."

The man grumbled. This was short notice. He ought to have been contacted earlier. As it was, he might not be able to rake up more than half a dozen of his Lofty Lads.

"That would be a pity, indeed to goodness," Apple said. "The Giants will have rather a lot of champagne left over."

Without grumble, the man promised to see what he could do.

Apple went to the bathroom. Mixing lipstick with soap, he coated his face and neck with pinkness. He finished up looking more normal than his usual pale self; also, the grazes and discolouration were less noticeable. After putting on the track suit top and woollen cap, he decided that he had changed his facial appearance enough for what should be a busy scene.

Apple went back to the telephone. He was sorry he hadn't

been able to start earlier. Theatrical agencies were all closed now. But there were other possibilities.

He called two suburban clubs for tall men, giving the story that a film was being shot at Paddington Station. "The director's looking for outsize extras. Lots of 'em. So if you and your friends can get there a few minutes before eight o'clock, there could be good-paying movie work for everyone."

There were no grumbles over the shortness of notice. Apple felt dreary about giving people false hopes like this. But he reminded himself that it was in a highly worthy cause—Tibor's safety and contented future, his mother's security.

Jane, Apple knew, would understand.

There were so many basketball clubs, leagues, and associations, that Apple hardly knew where to start. Amateur, professional, collegiate, military, church, local and county and national—the list was long. Finally he took them in order of size, the largest first, though he was mainly guessing at this. He kept each call brief: There were many more to be made.

Throughout, Apple used the same accent, one that he hoped would pass as American. He introduced himself as the public relations man for the Harlem Globetrotters. To collect money for charity, he said, the famous team of black athletes would be playing a running game of basketball through the streets of the Paddington district, starting at the railway station and ending in Hyde Park. The team who normally accompanied them on their world tours, to play as opponents, had missed a plane connexion. The Harlem Globetrotters would be alone.

"So," Apple said, "if you could possibly muster a few of the guys and get them to the station at eight o'clock, you'd be doing great things for charity, as well as for Anglo-American relations."

In each case, the response was eager, created, Apple knew, by the will to help a cause and the thrill of playing against a team with an international reputation. No one grumbled about short notice.

Apple went on calling until such grumbles would have been in order. While waiting for taxi-calling time, he practiced walking.

It was ten minutes before eight o'clock.

The cabbie, on Apple's directions, drew his taxi to a slow stop. They were right opposite the ramp that sloped down into the body of Paddington Station. A delivery van went down, a car came up. Rush hour long past, the traffic that passed between was meagre. It was still daylight.

"Listen," the cabbie said. "I can't park here for long." He didn't look back. He had done that once, when Apple had first got in, and had turned away again quickly.

"Hold on a minute or two more," Apple coaxed. "I'm waiting for someone."

"If it's someone from the station, we could wait down there just as easily."

"This is fine."

As the driver sighed nervously, a complaint without going too far, Apple looked in all directions. He was worried by the lack of action. He knew that some of those people whom he had called, being suspicious of a hoax, would have made a check, but he felt there should still be plenty who wouldn't.

Another van went down the ramp. Who's in that? Apple wondered. Goodies or baddies?

He noticed now, as the van turned from sight at the bottom, a man down there near the corner. In porter's uniform, he was sweeping. He would have looked a perfect part of the scene were it not for the fact that he worked with vigour, rather than the staunch languor of the British workingman. He had to be a phony.

"Now listen here, guv," the cabbie said.

Apple turned his head the other way at a burst of noise. He smiled with relief. Coming along on the other side, dressed in shorts and singlets, were eight or ten men. They were laughing boisterously. Not one of them was under six feet tall.

Apple pushed a pound note through to the driver. "Keep the change." He was getting out, on the curbside, manoeuvring his net of balls, when another taxi squealed to a stop behind. From it on the other side stepped five tall men. Their clothing was normal. The tallest of the group was close to seven and a half feet, and he put on an old-fashioned high-crown hat as he went with the others across the road to the ramp.

Apple followed on behind, clumping with care. At the ramp the basketball players joined on. They all went striding down together. The man in porter's uniform stopped sweeping and leaned weakly against the wall.

The mixed group turned into the concourse. It was crowded. In addition to the regular complement of transients, there seemed, to Apple, to be an unusual number of quietly dressed men standing by themselves and looking at nothing.

But that was only on the crowd's edge. Toward the centre, where Apple began to aim himself, the norm was abnormal. Most of the men were well above the six-foot mark. They were all ages, from pimply youths to a mammoth octogenarian; they were in all styles of dress, from brief, brightly coloured basketball outfits to business suits; they were of many races, from brown to pasty; they were of all builds, from super skinny to gross.

What the men all had in common, in addition to height, was a smile. It had the same character and lit every face. It stayed constant as its owner gazed about him, like a man who had just come home after a long absence.

Apple understood. He was smiling himself.

Pausing as he went by, a youth in a track suit of red gabardine grinned eye to eye with Apple and asked, "Have you seen the Harlem Globetrotters?"

"I heard they'd be here in five minutes."

"Good-o." He edged on through the crowd.

Apple noted the nonsmilers. Most had a legitimate reason for being put out at the hindrance of an unexpected, towering mob. Some had not. These were the quietly dressed men. If not standing, they circulated smoothly. If they looked only at people their own size, they were Tibor-seeking KGB, Apple knew, and he wondered if they found the lofty assembly strange, and analogous. If they looked at everyone of any size, they were British agents, seeking both the chemist and Appleton Porter.

Apple turned at a crash of music.

Coming through the swing doors that led to the Paddington Underground station, marching, was a brass band. The leader had a mace. He, like the others, wore a purple uniform with a shiny helmet and looked to be about eight feet tall.

The band was twenty strong. Behind it came more enormous men in civilian clothes. They carried a banner that announced the ensemble to be the London Lofty Lads.

Apple turned again, this time right around the other way. It was to avoid the eyes of a small man of around five feet eleven. He was searching the faces of everyone, tall or short.

Apple was now looking toward the railings that separated the concourse from the platforms. Streaming through the barrier, from a train that had recently arrived, were high and skinny West Indians in basketball dress.

Could that, Apple mused, have been the eight o'clock from

Uxbridge? As he began to work his way through the crowd, he glanced back toward the ramp. The pseudo-porter was still leaning on the wall. He was watching sad-eyed a passing file of towering men in yellow practice silks.

The noise was tremendous. The band boomed on, there were shouts from one corner where a game of passing had started, tall strangers yelled conversations at each other like old, deaf friends.

Apple had trouble with his balls. They kept knocking against people, though without disturbing the smiles. "Sorry," he constantly murmured, grinning. At last he slung the net of basketballs over his shoulder.

He decided not to ask at the barrier, now that he was close. He had been watching it, and Tibor hadn't passed through. The platform was empty. In any case, the porter on ticket-taking duty looked terrified; looked as if he might turn and run if any of the giants approached him.

A man tapped Apple's shoulder. "Know what time this Welsh lot's supposed to get here?" It, like the other question, was being asked all over.

"I don't know," Apple said. "Myself, I've come here for the smartest tall man competition."

The man smiled down at him. "Really?"

"The winner gets a hundred pounds."

"I'll have a bash at that." The man, in civvies, straightened his tie and moved away.

Apple followed, sifting into the crowd, aiming for a central position near the barriers. To be like everyone else, he asked a man where the movie company was. He needed to shout, fighting talk and the band.

The man yelled that he didn't know anything about a movie. "But maybe that's why somebody sent for the police."

"Police?"

"They're going around asking people what they're doing here."

Apple looked about with care. While doing so, he noted contentedly four taxis come off the ramp to unload a score of titans in shorts, more tall men come from the Underground station, and still more come hurrying in from another entrance. The concourse was getting packed.

Apple finally saw the constables. Or rather, he saw the silver tips of their helmets. The policemen were being dwarfed.

"Apple!"

He froze at the sound of the voice. It belonged, unmistakenly, to Tina Koves. It had come from somewhere behind him.

"Apple!" The shout was close now.

He half-turned to the side, hiding his face against the net of basketballs on his shoulder. People were looking past him. In that direction, in the corners of his eyes, Apple saw the blond Sickle. Seeming to be the size of a child in the soaring throng, she was coming straight toward him.

He made to go the other way; and halted. Approaching there, gaze switching from low to high, was one of the quietly dressed men. Apple began to move backwards. He stopped when Tina appeared. She had walked straight past him.

Tina went up to a man of about six feet seven. He was young, fair-haired, and had a full beard. His smile shot away when Tina reached up and tried to pull off the beard.

Apple couldn't hear the brief exchange that passed between the two. But as Tina moved on, heading for another man, this one with sunglasses, he heard her again call out, "Apple!"

He allowed her nine points for neat thinking. But, he mused, the KGB couldn't know for sure that he would be here—unless they had checked and definitely found out that the tall scene had been provoked, which would point the finger at Appleton Porter.

Apple looked at his watch. It told five minutes past eight. There was no sight or sound of a train, but more tall men were entering the station on all sides.

Apple turned at a polite, "Excuse me." Looking up at him was a police constable. He asked, "May I enquire as to your business here in the station, sir?"

"I'm waiting for my sister," Apple said. "She's coming in on the eight o'clock from Uxbridge."

Looking sour, the constable stepped away, to the next man, to whom he repeated his question. The man appeared to be close to nine feet tall in a cowboy hat. He said:

"I'm trying to get a job in the movies."

"That story isn't true, sir, about a film being made here and the director looking for extras."

"It isn't?"

"No, sir. I'll have to ask you to vacate the premises at once."

Apple slid away. Ten points to old Angus, he thought. It didn't take him long to think of a way to trim the crowd. But it was going to take some doing. And wouldn't be effective unless Tibor's train was more late than the average.

Apple stopped. He had seen Nick Stick.

The clown was moving through the crowd. He wore a new looking lounge suit. It fitted him the way a thimble fits a pin. His eyes were darting in all directions.

Of course, Apple mused, they would have to bring Nick Stick in on this end of the business. He was one of the few, along with Tina, who knew the missing Hungarian well. He also knew the market gardener.

Watching from around the net of balls balanced on his shoulder, Apple had seen a smile flick on and off Nick Stick's face. It happened again now. Even the KGB are human, Apple thought, but he steeled himself against sympathy.

He also had to steel himself against the noise. The concourse was packed. More players had joined in the corner game. Part of the crowd sang along with the brass band, which was booming out a tune from the top twenty. Everyone talked in shouts.

Apple looked at his watch. Ten minutes past eight.

A man six inches taller than Apple's present self brushed by. The net of basketballs was dislodged. Apple grabbed at it hurriedly, managed to hold it in place. But the movement had drawn the attention of Nick Stick. He looked, frowned, looked again.

Apple turned away. He began to ease through the crowd. Seconds later, glancing back, he saw that the clown was swiftly following. The smile he wore now was of a different nature.

Apple had not, he felt, been positively identified. Nick could be making the same number of tries as Tina. But that wasn't the only problem. If the KGB were anywhere near him when Tibor arrived, he would have to avoid the chemist.

Apple saw the man who had spoken to the policeman after himself. He surged toward him, beckoned him close, shouted at close range, with urgency, "Still want a job in the movies?"

"Too right."

"The director's here now. Chap back there in the new suit. He's coming this way. Face like a skull. See him?"

"Gotcha," the man said. "Thanks."

He and Apple moved with the same determination in different directions. Apple stopped again by a giant black in a dazzling green track suit. He told him that Nick Stick was the racist responsible for the hoax.

"What hoax?"

"About the Harlem Globetrotters supposedly going to appear here."

"Oh that," the black said. "I'm here for the Mister Tall, Dark, and Handsome competition."

"He's responsible for that hoax as well," Apple said, moving on.

The next two men he spoke to, in ordinary clothes, he gave them the film director story. To two more he said they could get tickets from Nick Stick for the supper that was being laid on for the Welsh visitors.

Apple looked back. He could no longer see the clown. He stopped and was glad to be able to do so. For one thing, he didn't like drawing attention to himself with the hustle. For another, he didn't want to leave this section close to the barriers. For a third thing, sweat under the soap-lipstick mixture was making his face itch.

Taking off his scarlet cap, Apple let it fall unnoticed to the floor: change of image from last sighting. He knew it would have been better to try and give the cap to someone, set a red herring, but he might get involved.

A mite of six feet three asked him, "Do you know who the judges are in this competition?"

Apple sent him off with a description of Nick Stick.

He held the net of basketballs down at his side. Their use, like the cap's, was over, but Apple was reluctant to discard them because he liked having something to grip.

He tensed. He could hear a train whistle. It and a voice from the loudspeakers came faintly above the bedlam. This has to be it, Apple thought. This must be Tibor's train.

He moved, making to go closer to the barriers. Smiling, he circled around a trio of giants who were shouting smilingly about the rumour of a hoax.

Apple felt his arm taken in a hard grip. He looked around sharply; then down. A small, quietly dressed man was beside him. He looked, with his blandness of feature, like a clerk on his way home from work.

He said, mouthing the words against the noise, "Angus Watkin would like a chat with you."

It was the agent from Oxford Street, Apple realized, the one who had been used because of his speciality of sleight-of-hand. Apple hissed urgently:

"I'm busy. Go away. You'll spoil everything."

It wasn't Watkin's invented, unwritten law that had brought the man here, Apple recognised, but the fact that he was one of the few in the Service who had had a recent, close-up, real-life look at the tall renegade.

Apple repeated, "Go away."

The arm grip tightened. The agent needed his glory too. He said, "Watkin's upstairs in the bar of the station hotel. Come on."

"Give me ten minutes." The train was coming in.

"Sorry," the man lied. He added, "You've been pulled out."

"Okay," Apple said. "I'll go." He moved off, away from the barriers, beyond which he could see the approaching train. The grip stayed on his arm. He was thinking busily. He shook his head when the agent said, "Don't try anything."

"Why should I? I'm only here to see the wrap-up."

"Sure you are, Russet. That's why you set this scene with all these bloody freaks."

Apple stared down at him coldly. "I know what I'm doing." He could hear the train slowing.

"What's that you say?"

The racket was impossible. Apple shook his head. But then he himself asked, "What's that you say?" He looked closely at the man as he mouthed, "I said it was all unnecessary."

Watkin had used the same expression. "Why?"

"Because," the agent said, "Tibor Polk's mother has been dead for three months."

Apple stopped. He gazed all around the roof and then back at the man. He asked, "Are you sure?"

"The final proof came through this morning. The Soviets have been sending Polk phony letters."

"Well, well, well," Apple said, slowly and heavily, released. "So Tibor has nothing to worry about."

"Right."

Apple mouthed, "Except getting snatched by his own people."

"They're outnumbered two to one."

"But they know what he looks like, and nobody here in the Service does." He smiled. "Except me."

The agent shook his head. "What's that you say?"

Apple lifted the net of balls. He tossed it high in the air, at the same time sagging at the knees to yell, "Catch!"

The man, his nerves obviously tuned to a fine hair trigger, reacted immediately. He released the arm grip and jerked both hands upward. Apple gave him a mighty shove that sent him staggering, turned and surged into the crowd.

"And what's more," he said to nobody, "I'm going to be the one who brings him in."

The train had stopped. Evidently assuming it to be carrying the expected people, whether Welsh or American or whatever, part of the crowd started cheering, there was a general movement toward the barriers, and the band switched to playing full blast the hymn of its members, "Nearer My God to Thee."

Apple found himself caught up in the movement. He was carried along. The tall wave took him toward where people, genuine greeters, were waiting by the barrier railings. Eyes round, they began to move to the sides. Some remained.

One of these was Nick Stick.

The clown, his suit less new looking than before, was darting sharp, grim glances. Far back behind him, passengers were getting out of the train and coming along the platform.

Steadily and surely, Apple was being carried on. The men around him were happy and determined. With communication almost nil, they shouted at each other about basketball and Welsh giants, film crews and competition judges. The clamour was awesome.

Apple lowered his head and kept his face tilted down. He made himself just tall enough to see ahead. He wanted to keep out of sight of Nick Stick, who, seeing him coming this way, would surely guess that Tibor was on the train.

The crowd took Apple on. The clogged pores of his face itched for the freedom to sweat that everywhere else on his body was having. He thought he might well be on the verge of being stricken with claustrophobia.

That made him straighten.

He was spotted by the clown.

Hopelessly, Apple stared back, as if to show that he was someone else, or to will the other man into thinking he was. He even shook his head, though unaware of the act.

A crafty, knowing look came into Nick Stick's eyes. As though in answer to Apple's headshake, he nodded. Turning quickly, he pushed by the ticket collector and went onto the platform.

"Stop!" Apple shouted, which was double pointless, for he could hardly hear his voice himself.

The human wave, almost there, slowed: Passengers were coming through the barrier. The wave stopped and split: Passengers were making their way through.

Groaning, Apple was carried away to one side. He tried to

resist. It was impossible. The mass was implacable and powerful. He was slowly being taken further and further away from the barrier, from the platform, and from Tibor.

Don't fight it, he told himself abruptly. Go with the mob. Get around to the platform another way. Go over the tracks, underneath the train.

Apple managed to turn himself about. He began to push through. The going was easier in this direction. Men were willing to trade places, get up front.

Forging on, aiming for the crowd's edge, Apple tried not to think of Tibor being seen by Nick Stick, being told by him that he was British Intelligence, being led willingly off to the Iron Curtain's local fold. Once there, he would never again have a chance at gaining freedom.

Apple pushed and squirmed. He forced himself to smile as he waded through the smilers and cheerers and singers. To himself he insisted that Tibor would avoid being seen by anyone whom he recognised, except his new friend.

The crowd thinned. Apple, twisting this way and that, was able to stride. He cut toward the platform-end railings, where he came into a patch of space. He dashed to the nearest barrier.

Next, he was staggering sideways toward the rails. A man, quietly dressed, had butted him in the ribs. By grabbing the railings Apple kept himself upright. He turned. The man was on him immediately.

Short and stocky, crew-cutted, hard-faced, the attacker gave his trade away by his crouching stance, his rigidly flat hands. One of the latter chopped at a forearm, the other would have jabbed an eye if the victim had been smaller.

Gagging at the pain in his arm, Apple shot foldingly downward from the hips. He tupped with the top of his brow. The man was hit full in the face. His nose starting to spurt blood, he went weaving away backwards.

Apple, dazed, made again for the barrier. The man was faster and in less awkward footwear. He got there first and turned on Apple with a blood-spitting snarl.

They grappled. While defending himself from chops, Apple used the only weapon he had: his superior height and weight. He leaned over the man while pressing down.

"Break that up!"

Apple found himself being wrenched back. The interruptors were two policemen. Tough and fierce, they held Apple firmly by the arms. One asked what the hell he thought he was playing at, the other said to the bleeding man:

"Are you all right, sir?"

Apple shook his head, tried to speak, gestured helplessly toward the platforms, tried to move. The hold on both arms was solid. He gasped, "Train."

Holding a hand to his bloody face, ignoring the policeman, the man backed off. He swung away and went into the crowd.

Apple managed, "Quick. Help me. Get me to platform five."

"What's your hurry?"

"I'm meeting someone. From Uxbridge. No time to lose." He pulled. His arms came free from the double grip. He stepped away.

"That's a lie for a start," one of the policemen said. "Uxbridge trains come in downstairs, not up here."

Apple stopped. He turned back. "What's that, officer?"

"Uxbridge, mate, is on the Underground."

Apple stared for only another second. He burst off into a stooping, clumping run. The policemen didn't try to stop him. He cursed the boots as he dodged in and out of the people who were making up the crowd's edge.

Apple darted through the basketless ball game, charged through the middle of the blasting brass band, slipped around behind a newspaper stand when he spotted Tina by its front, stumped on as fast as he could toward the swing doors.

He went through, pushing by a group of tall men who were puffingly late. He went along a passage, clumped his way down an escalator, came into the lower, smaller station.

Tibor was there.

Capless, his coat lying open, the chemist stood patiently by a ticket machine.

Approaching at a stumbling run, Apple waved.

Tibor suddenly turned the other way. He ran. He sped to a turnstile, which, with surprising agility, he vaulted. He ran to an escalator, his coat-tails flying out behind him.

"It's me!" Apple yelled, still moving. His words floated off and died. "It's your friend Apple!"

Tibor had sunk from view.

With a fast run-up, Apple threw himself into a high jump to clear the turnstile. His toe caught on the far side. He pitched over, shot to the floor, landed on his arms, kept going in a roll.

He finished up by the escalator. Rising unsteadily, he went onto the moving stairs. Tibor was midway down, still running. He didn't glance back at the shout of his name.

Riskily on the high heels, Apple went down in long leaps. He covered five or six steps at a time. Each landing was a trauma. He had to hold his balance sideways, he needed to stop himself from shooting forward head first, he had to stand the pain of the jolt.

But he was close behind the older man as Tibor leapt over the bottom of the escalator. With two yards of space between them, they chased along a tunnel. It was a race that Apple could have won easily without the hindering boots. He didn't waste time and breath on another shout.

They came out onto a platform. It was deserted. No train, no people. Tibor dribbled to a halt. Apple, exhausted and bemused, did the same. The last repeated echo of their footfalls died away. It was quiet.

Tibor flapped his arms against his sides. He turned and said, "The train's gone."

Apple panted, "It's me."

Tibor nodded absently. "You were a little late. I expected that. I was not concerned. I knew that you would be busy getting everything neatly arranged." He squared his shoulders. "I am ready to be kidnapped."

"Good," Apple said. He sagged in pain and weariness, in joy and triumph. "But I'll explain upstairs in the hotel bar."

Tibor lowered his eyes sheepishly. "I am sorry about the cap," he said. "The one you bought me."

"What?"

"I forgot it. I left it on the train."

EPILOGUE

Two days later, in a bustling cafeteria near Baker Street, Apple was sitting at a table with Angus Watkin. They sat at their ease. To anyone bored enough to give them a second glance, the two men would have passed for office people taking the eleven o'clock coffee break.

Apple wore his usual clothes, had his usual neatness, and apart from a slight discolouration about the face looked altogether his usual self. Inside, however, he was older and happier and more confident.

Angus Watkin aligned his spoon. He said, "No doubt you will soon get to the reason why you requested this meeting."

"I was wondering if we were safe here."

"Overcaution, Porter, can be as damaging as carelessness."

"Yes, sir."

All was well between Apple and his superior. In the hotel bar, when the fuss had died down, Apple had explained aside to Watkin about the station scene.

The KGB, he said, had arranged for the tall men to be there so that Tibor would be confused. He himself had shown himself openly on the concourse, without hat or disguise, only adding to his height to make it *seem* that he was trying to change his appearance, so that the KGB would see him and therefore not think of looking downstairs. He was risking his skin, Apple said, but he had done it. He denied having received an order to step out. He mentioned the unwritten law.

Angus Watkin had been too pleased at having the chemist in his hands to give more than a token complaint; which pleasure he had shown by stroking a forefinger across his chin.

Now he looked into his coffee cup. "Filthy stuff," he said. "But I mustn't ramble on. You were about to enlighten me, Porter."

Apple said, as if he hadn't heard, "By the way, sir, I can't speak too highly of the operative in charge of the dive-bomber. The way she found me in the countryside was quite brilliant."

"You did tell me that already."

"Yes. And how is my friend Tibor?"

"Mr. Polk is quite well," Watkin said through a faint sigh. "We had a nice long chat yesterday. He is, naturally, upset about his mother, but otherwise fine."

"I'm glad."

"After a thorough debriefing, he will be available for a short time to visitors."

"Is he at Damian House?"

Angus Watkin turned his head away casually. It meant no comment. It also meant that his patience was running out.

But Apple was unsure of the gamble he had planned on trying, the one he thought of as his swimming-pool ploy. While thinking it out he had felt marvellously smooth and corrupt, the old pro to the last degree.

He asked himself now, however, if it were possible for him to be punished in some supranormal way for the dishonesty. Apple had a vague belief in retribution.

He stalled again, saying, "Since I was so deeply involved in this mission, sir, I hope you won't think me out of line if I ask why you were so willing to accept Soma-2." The wording had the correct amount of crawl.

Watkin turned back. "It was simply that the Soviets must, patently, have an antidote. Which was fine with us. We could feed their antidoted agents misinformation while they were supposedly under the influence."

"Really, sir? How, sir?"

"By talking among ourselves. By saying, in effect, it doesn't matter what we discuss because he won't remember it afterwards."

"Of course. Brilliant, sir."

Angus Watkin asked, "Quite sure there's nothing else, before you get to the nub?"

"Nothing," Apple said. He decided to go ahead and start on his swimming pool.

Speaking in a lower voice, Apple explained about his invented suspicions of Arvo, the Finnish strong-man, who had talked oddly about the Soviet Union, which he had admitted in confidence to having visited several times and not exactly as a tourist.

"He confided in me, sir," Apple said, "after he heard me use a Russian expression. He thinks I'm a fellow-traveller."

"Indeed?"

"Yes, sir. Absolutely. So what I thought, sir, was this. I could rejoin the circus for a few weeks, feel out the Finn, see what develops. Don't you think that's a good idea, sir?"

Watkin looked at him carefully. "Rejoin the circus, mm?"

Apple was almost certain he could see a gleam in his superior's eyes; and he read it as failure. It had been a mistake, of course, to protest so much about Jane's cleverness. He should never have mentioned her after that first time in the hotel bar.

Watkin said, "Quite an interesting suggestion, Porter."

Apple could hardly believe it. Was even old Angus human after all?—he thought. That lasted scant seconds. The gleam was not for romance, Apple told himself, but for the possibility of another feather for the Watkin hat. Motive Apple didn't care about. He waited and hoped.

"Yes, very well," Angus Watkin said at length. "I'll set it up with Sir Jasper. If you call in tomorrow, I'll have details for you."

"Thank you, sir," Apple said limply.

"Prepare to go two days from now. That will be a week after you took Soma-2. You were told you'd be a little thirsty, I understand. The other agent who took it is fine."

Apple could tell from his superior's manner that Tibor hadn't yet made it clear that he would not be working on any more drug projects. That was his major reason for wanting to escape to the West. There would be no more Soma-2, and its antidote would never appear. Watkin was in for a shock, Apple thought, happily.

He said, "I'm glad you go for my idea, sir."

"It might be useful to see what the Finn's stand is, even if it's only political *katasak*."

"*Katasak*, sir? That's a new one on me."

"A Hungarian word I got from Mr. Polk," Watkin said. "It means impotence. More exactly, sexual impotence." He put his hands on the table and rose. "I must be off."

Apple also got up. "Well, good-bye, sir."

"Good morning, Porter."

"I trust you will be pleased with our latest defector's contributions," Apple said. He smiled politely.

"And for my part, I trust you will do your best at the circus," Watkin said. He smiled politely.